The Elven Monarchy Scribes:

Book 1

Forgotten Magic

H.L. Lafferty

Ladies
of the
Lakes
Publishing

"HAPPINESS COMES WHEN YOU WORK
HARD DOING WHAT YOU LOVE."

H.L. LAFFERTY

TABLE OF CONTENTS

~Chapter 1 ~

Discoveries

The chill of a breeze caught Alveen by surprise. Her vision unrevealing to the scene around her and an eerie silence gave way to the quiet noise of the gravel beneath her feet. Another gust of wind blew the clouds away from the full moon, allowing it to illuminate what she now saw as a seaside town. She didn't recognize where she was. and she didn't see anyone walking the gloomy cobblestone streets even with the street lamps revealing everything around her even more clearly. In the distance, waves lapped along the stone shoreline.

Slowly she stepped towards the walkway. "What are you doing?!" she heard a frantic whisper from one of the nearby buildings. Stopping to look, she still saw no one. A scream in the distance caused her heart to race, her head instinctively snapped towards the cry for help. Alveen walked faster toward the call, someone needed her. Rounding the corner towards an old rickety pier, she froze in her steps. A little girl's body lay limp on the creaky wooden planks and beside her lifeless form was a creature unlike anything she had ever seen or heard of, which was saying a lot since her brother taught her mythology.

She instinctively wanted to call it a centaur as it had the upper body of what seemed like a man, and the lower of not a horse, but possibly a dragon? It had talons that scraped the ground with every step and a long scale covered tail with spined fins along the dorsal side. An oversized translucent fin snapped open and closed at the end of it. As she inspected further she noticed it's hands were webbed and the scales extended upward onto the torso . Her heart was still racing, she hadn't been able to save the little girl.

A sorrow filled sob caught in her throat and time stopped. She covered her mouth before any sound could escape but it had already heard her. She stood and started taking what she thought were silent steps backwards but she couldn't take her eyes off what she saw. Neon yellow eyes met hers set atop a protruding lower jawbone full of fangs that looked like they were most certainly used for shredding flesh. The skin was an off green color from what she could see in light given off by the street

lamps that surrounded them. It dripped a slime that she could
only assume was giving off the stench that wrapped around her.
Seaweed like dreadlocks covered its head and hung over the
rippling muscles in the creatures torso. There was no way she
could defend herself against this monster in front of her.
Suddenly it stopped. She continued backing up. It tilted its head
and gave a malicious grin. It's voice rumbled her very being,

"What a prize I've found today. The sorceress will be
pleased." The sorceress? What is going on? Alveen was brought to
an abrupt halt in her reverse escape when she ran into someone.
Ice cold hands wrapped around her biceps, squeezing tighter than
what she could call comfortable. She tried to turn around but was
forced to the ground by her assailant. Pain radiated down through
her head as it made contact with the cobblestone walkway. With
blurry vision she turned to try to look at her attacker, only
catching a glimpse of the hem of a teal and gold gown trailing the
ground by her face before she went unconscious.

She woke in a cold sweat, breathing heavy. This was a
reoccurring dream she had only recently begun to have and it
always woke her in the middle of the night. She reached over for
her alarm clock, it was 6am. She decided it was best to just get her
day started as she swung her legs over the side of her bed.
Stretching was something she made a religious habit of every
morning.

Since it was still so early, though the sun was above the horizon, she walked down the staircase and toward the back porch of her brother's immaculate home. When she got there she reached down for the bow and quiver that hung on custom rack just inside the back door. She did not have many friends, but the few that she did were avid outdoorsmen and had taught her about fishing, hunting and survival skills. She was often invited to go rock climbing, hiking and rappelling with them. Most her of time she spent with her face in a book or her laptop as she wrote stories the world would never see.

She paced out thirty yards from her target, perfected her stance and she drew back the string on her compound bow. She regulated her breathing and released her first arrow, landing perfectly in the center. She smiled to herself, impressed with her first shot. As she continued her first set, she noticed was not as consistent as she had hoped. She paced out again and shot five more sets until her shoulder began to shake. She knew when she needed to stop, and this was her limit. Retrieving her arrows quickly and placing her equipment back on the rack she decided to make her way upstairs to get ready for her day.

After she took a shower she spent some time debating what she would wear. It wasn't an important day in any way. She worked in an office setting by the collage, but she did enjoy putting an effort into her appearance. Standing in front of her mirror in her elegantly themed bathroom, she admired herself.

Her blonde spiral curls hung to the bottom of her rib cage, holding the curl even as she ran her fingers through the locks. Quickly, she splashed water on her face and put a small amount of lotion on. The color in her cheeks was rosy. Her eyes were a rare shade she had been told. Bright teal shined in her irises, rimmed around the edges with a distinctive golden hue. Her figure was athletic, though you couldn't see it under her oversized t-shirt she slept in. She wore little makeup around her eyes and on her lips making her look a little more awake. Sifting through her closet she pulled on a knee length black pencil skirt and a burgundy blouse tucked into it. She slipped into silky black flats and accented with golden earrings and a statement necklace. Walking to her bathroom she approved her look and headed to the kitchen to make breakfast for her and Zakarian. He spent more time on his appearance than she did which allowed her the time to make pineapple blueberry smoothies for the two of them and clean up the mess before he even walked into the kitchen.

The day seemed to fly by when it came time to meet Zakarian and head back to the house for the day. She had done data entry all day. It kept her from dealing face to face with customers but staring at a computer for hours left her exhausted.

"What do you say to a few rounds of cribbage tonight? Mentally challenge yourself a little?" Zakarian requested on the drive home.

"That sounds like a fine idea." She changed into grey sweatpants and a university t-shirt before she joined Zakarian in the lavish dining room. He dealt the first hand to begin the first of three rounds of the card game.

"HA! I won again. You are truly horrible at this." Zakarian's voice echoed through the large historical dining room as he playfully claimed his victory over Alveen once again. Alveen enjoyed card and board games, unlike many of her age. She was intelligent beyond the average young adult. Her mind held a passion for discoveries and for the truth behind everything. She enjoyed interactions like these, compared to cell phones and computers. Technology was never something she took much advantage of.

"Yes, yes. You've won again. How shall I repay my losing's this time, brother?" Zakarian sat back in his dark red velvet upholstered chair. The back extended so high you would have mistaken it for a throne. The home they lived in was scattered with historical furniture and knick-knacks. The couple that owned it last were wealthy and they filled their home with exciting and educational pieces that left guests wondering about the item's past. Alveen watched Zackarian as he pretended this was a hard decision. Finally, he answered.

"Alright, well since you've lost all three times I believe you owe me dinner. You must make this dinner, no going out." Alveen smiled and rolled her eyes as she headed towards the kitchen. Zakarian began to clean up the cards and board. She was a very skilled cook and it helped that she enjoyed having her nose stuck between the pages of a book because she always made everything perfectly from any recipe book, which they had a shelf full of. They placed bets on all the games they played. Sometimes they had to buy the other ice cream, other times they had to clean something or tell a secret. Today, dinner was the wager.

Going to the pantry she pulled out her tan and grey apron tying it around her waist and behind her neck. Pulling the ponytail holder off her wrist she reached back and made a quick messy bun with her blonde curls so she could start on her next masterpiece. It wasn't long before she decided on a chicken Caesar salad, homemade bread sticks and balsamic glazed steak rolls. Looking up at the oversized clock on the wall she noted that it was about three thirty when she started, giving her plenty of time to make everything.

As the baking was coming close to being complete, she finished the last of the cleaning and set the table. She elegantly plated the dishes and called for Zakarian to join her.

"You will never fail to impress me with your skills in the kitchen Alveen. This is magnificent!" Zakarian boasted as he took his first bite, bursting with flavor from the seasoning she mixed together and the juices she masterfully preserved inside. He made approving noises as he tried the breadsticks and salad.

"I am pretty amazing, aren't I? I'm glad it turned out this delicious."

"You are going to need to teach me how to cook like this someday. Who knows, I may marry someone who is no good at cooking."

"You can just hire me as your personal chef! Then I don't have to get some horrible job."

"Good possibility." He laughed responding to her suggestion. Zakarian was a classy man and Alveen admired his elegance. He always had a nice clean haircut, a clean shaven face that allowed his sharp jaw to show. Ninety percent of the time he wore suits or at least a suit jacket. He was a professor at the local college teaching courses on legends and lore. Alveen was fascinated by it all and whenever possible she would sit in on his lectures.

Zakarian was the only parental figure she had, but he was also her best friend. He understood her mind and passions deeper than just skimming the surface of a person's character. She had never known her parents but Zakarian always said it was for the better. He removed her from a harmful home situation when she was very little. He was quite a bit older than her though, turning thirty this year. She often thought about how life would be different if she grew up with both parents like a normal teenager.

She made her way to her bedroom. Often, she spent some time looking out at the stars before she climbed into bed. It was something that made her remember how truly small she was. Struggling, she opened the old window allowing the warm breeze to flood into her room. She climbed between her covers, snuggling them close to her face.

Alveen rose at six in the morning, grateful she had a dreamless sleep. The breeze from her open window brushed across her skin as she stretched her arms out walking towards her closet. Her room was not that of a teenage girl, as would be expected. A large oak desk with detailed moldings along the sides sat on the far side of her room opposite her bed facing a large window that overlooked the back yard. On it was a pile of notebooks, scrap paper, pens, pencils, picture frames that held photos of her and Zakarian. All of her pictures were more recent; none of them reflecting their childhood. One side of her room was full of book shelves that were already built into the room and now were overflowing with stories and knowledge she had started accumulating. Her bed was a colossal disorder of her neutral colored covers and sheets, no bold colors or patterns on any area of her room. She was simple and she was logical. After an hour of deciding on an outfit and making her hair and makeup presentable she emerged from her room.

She wasn't involved with much outside of work and home so most of the time she just walked over to Zakarian's lecture hall when she finished work and waited for him.

"Did you learn anything today?" He asked as he walked up the stairs in the lecture hall to sit by her after the students vacated.

"Hm, I wouldn't say I learned much, but I was thoroughly entertained." She stated with a sarcastic smile. As much as she enjoyed the lectures and enjoyed learning about the legends and lore, she didn't actually believe very much of it.

"Hey, this is my life's work here." A laugh escaped his throat as he shook his head at his sister's stubbornness. "You are very reasonable, so why is it so hard for you to have an open mind sometimes? You know there is a lot this world hasn't discovered and a lot they never will."

"I'll believe it when I see it. Maybe all of this is real, but until I go making crazy statements like such, I'd like to see it for myself." They walked to his car and drove back home. Their home was out of town about five minutes, just far enough that no one bothered them. The driveway was stretched out over about half a mile through the woodlands that encompassed the property making their home impossible to see if you were just driving by.

As they pulled into view of the historical building. They exchanged curious glances. A white SUV was parked in front of their garage and a tall dark-haired man leaned against the back hatch as if he were waiting for them.

"Do you know him?"

"Yes." He said in a mono tone, but he didn't add anything about whom the man was. "Stay here please."

"Should I be worried?"

"No, not at all." He managed to smile when he answered that time. Zakarian got out of the car and walked towards the man. Alveen couldn't hear their conversation once Zakarian closed his door.

"Well, you've aged slightly haven't you? Still look brilliant though I must say. I figured this world would have more of an effect on you." The stranger spoke to him as he approached.

"Nice to see you too, Samual." He smirked and hugged the man. Alveen watched from the car. The man was a little taller than Zakarian and had the same clean look he did. His dark hair was standing up in a stylish mess and he wore a navy suit, over a white dress shirt with a satin black tie that reflected his shining black dress shoes. She couldn't hear anything they were saying but it seemed to be going well. "What are you doing here?"

"Well, hello to you. How have you been the last twelve years? How's grandmother?" Samual joked at his straight forwardness. "I was sent to bring you two home. Your grandmother is missing you and unfortunately situations are not lightening any. She insists that you are to be brought home."

"Situations aren't getting any better and she insists we go back!? What sense does that make. We are here to protect Alveen. I can't take her back to that."

"You haven't told her anything have you?" Zakarian hesitated before he answered,

"No. She had no reason to know."

"Well now she does. This is her life too, her family, her destiny. And you want to keep her from that? Have you seen this world? I'm surprised she's not dead already! No offense to you of course. "

"None taken." Zakarian paused, thinking of how to go about this unexpected situation. Alveen knew nothing of her true past. She knew nothing of her parents, or of her culture and heritage. She was going to be furious and would probably not believe any of it anyways. "Fine. Go in the house. I'll meet you in the library." Samual bowed slightly and headed for the front door. Alveen was relieved when she saw that this man was a friend and no one to be feared.

"So, who is he?" She asked excitedly when Zakarian came back to turn off the car. They didn't have a lot of guests over. Every now and then they had a classy party for Zakarian's co-workers, but that was the extent of it. Zakarian sighed.

"He's an old friend of mine and our family." He was now standing at the passenger door as she climbed out. Alveen could feel that he was having a hard time trying to find the words he needed to continue this conversation. "What I'm about to explain to you, please let me finish before you interrupt or ask questions. This is a very delicate situation and I've been wrong in keeping much of this from you. Come on." He guided her into the house.

Alveen was hopelessly confused and that was not something she felt very often. Slowly she followed Zakarian to the library where the dark haired man stood scanning over the papers on the desk. "Okay, now what's going on?" She exclaimed impatiently. The man was leaned back against the desk near the far side of the room with his arms crossed over his chest, resting his chin in one hand with a bent finger over his lips that held an eager smile like he knew something she didn't. She wasn't one to notice a man's appearance, but he pulled off a suit very well.

"Alveen, this is Samual. He is a very old friend of our family and he's here to take us home." He paused to see if she was going to say anything. She held her tongue as he had requested. "Our home is not exactly what I've made you believe it was, nor is our family situation. We are..." He paused, she had never seen him have such a hard time with words. She would never believe a word he would say, no matter how he thought about phrasing it.

"You're royalty. You're mother and father may possibly be dead. Your grandmother is on the throne and wishes that the two of you return to Beannaithe to prepare for training and reconnect with your culture. You were sent here when you were young to keep you both protected, being heirs to the throne and with the threat to your home lands growing, but it is now apparent to her that if they over take the throne and you are not

there to stop it and reclaim the throne, your world is lost."
Samual blurted out quickly with an amused look on his face. He
studied Alveen. She was taking everything in, certain this was
simply a joke. She studied the newcomer, trying to decipher his
stare.

"Ummm, I'm not sure how to react." She stated, but she
played along to see what they were going on about. "Where
exactly are we from?" She questioned Zakarian.

"Beannaithe." He paused then realized she was waiting
for more details, "It's a world not much different than this one in
many aspects. Also one where everything I've been teaching on, is
in some variation, true. I decided to teach legends and lore when
we arrived here because I had experience with everything it taught,
only much of it is not true on this world."

"You keep saying 'this world'. . . as in another planet or
dimension?" As much as Alveen wanted to interject and call
bogus on everything they said, she wanted to hear everything out
as well. A large portion of her believed this was simply just a way
for Zakarian to open her mind.

"More like portals that take you outside this galaxy,
where simple things like time are not even the same. You see the
extremely shortened version of this is that you are from a royal

line on Beannaithe. You are the only race that is able to harness the magic within the planet and conjure up the types of portals that are safely able to be traveled through, bringing you to distant lands like where we are now." Samual laughed out loud when Alveen's face turned to pure disbelief. "I bet he hasn't told you about your abilities either? Or what race you are exactly?" Samual's face turned to pure joy. He outstretched one of his arms and twisted his hand is a very elegant fashion. Alveen followed his gaze and saw the books from her shelves levitating off the shelves and moving around the room. He moved one of them to her lap and continued to move his hands and then, what she assumed was his form of showing off, he crossed his arms again and kept moving them around the room. "You have the same abilities I do. You are of elven decent."

"This is so. ..." She couldn't find the word, thinking it could just be some impressive illusion. "Wait... elven.. As in elf? I'm an elf? I thought elves were small with pointed ears." Zakarian finally stepped in after Samual had done his dirty work.

"Is this proof enough for you? And yes. We are elves. Elves are like the monarchy where we are from. Or at least pure bloods are. Many elves are only very small percentage so. For example; Samual here is not pure of blood, though he has sat at the Monarchy's side for many centuries now. He is only ninety percent elf, ten percent witch, or warlock I should say. His magic comes from both the elements, from his elven side, and from mixtures and potions, from his warlock side. So some of his magic is done naturally, as he just showed, but something things, healing for example, can only be done with precious potions or mixtures unless you are pure blood like us. *You* are all elf. You have the magic naturally within you and you can draw it out from the elements, but I've never had you attempt anything like that. So as far as you've been aware, you are normal, for lack of a better term." He took a deep breath and stared at her, hoping she wouldn't be upset.

"What about our parents? You said they might be dead? They were thought to be alive this whole time? Where are they?" She stood up looking between Zakarian and Samual for answers.

"We aren't sure. Before you left your mother went missing. No one knows where she went, or if she ever survived. After you left, your father was falling apart. He had just lost all three of you. Less than a year later, his house went up in flames. His body was never found. So, in all honesty, I have no idea where your parents are or what became of them if they are still alive." Samual's voice was somber this time when he spoke. "They were like parents to me as well. Zakarian and I grew up together and my mother is unfortunately a very well-known witch fighting with the Dorcha tribes."

"Dorcha tribes?" Alveen asked.

"The tribes that live in the valleys. They are cruel and have been trying to over throw the throne for years. They are the reason we were sent away." Zakarian explained. All was quiet for a long period of time as Alveen took everything in.

"So you lied. All these years you've been lying to me." She looked into Zakraians eyes with hurt. The one person she swore she could trust with her life, had been lying to her and she never even realized it. It wasn't her lineage or forgotten world she was upset about, but the truth about her parents that really caused her distress.

"To be fair, he was doing all of this to protect you. It wasn't his choice to leave." Samual tried defending his best friend. "But we really must leave, soon." She pondered his request, continuing to play along, assuming she would unravel their bluff soon enough.

"I'm ready to go. What do I all need to bring with me?" She asked quietly, still nearly expecting them to end the charade. Samual and Zakarian exchanged looks and Samual went to wait in the car.

"Just bring one bag if you need it. Most of the necessities will be there, but you can bring anything that might be sentimental." She went to her room without speaking another word to him. It didn't take long for her to pack. She grabbed a backpack and put a few of her favorite books and a pile of notebooks, a few outfits, hygiene products and quickly stuffed writing supplies in the pockets. She stood in her doorway, backpack slung over her shoulder and she paused, looking back at what she had known to be her home and the room she found comfort in. Who knows, maybe she would be back and this was all just a joke. She descended the stairs heading straight for the car.

"Ready Your Highness?" Samual said and he opened the rear door for her to climb in.

"Your Highness? What are you, a medieval knight?" She commented, intentionally trying to sound rude. He gave her a smirk, meeting her stare for a moment.

"Something like that." He said before closing the door. She had no idea where they were going but she really didn't want to ask any more questions at the moment. As much as she didn't want to acknowledge Samual, she was just now seeing how tall he was. He had to be over six feet tall because he towered over her athletic five foot nine form. She was still feeling like this was all a dream

• • •

and she was just giving into Zakarian's comments about her being too closed minded.

She must have fallen asleep during the car ride because when she woke up they were at a small airport. The sound of car doors closing had woke her up. Samual and Zakarian headed for the back of the SUV.

"Where in the world are we and where are we going?" She finally let her curiosity get the best of her. How long were they going to play at this?

"We're going to Ireland!" Samual yelled from behind the car. He was moving the few bags her and Zakarian had brought with into a plane. Actually it looked more like a private jet. She gave Zakarian a confused look.

"There is a mountain there that holds a tremendous amount of magic. Enough for Samual and I to open a portal long enough for all three of us to return home." She just nodded that she understood and then leaned against the door when she stepped out of the vehicle. *Oh, going to Ireland to find a magical mountain to portal ourselves across the universe? Yea, what's weird about that?*

"After you" Samual smiled as he led her to the staircase. As she stepped onto the jet she felt as if she was hit with a pillow of luxury. The jet had seats on each side of it facing towards the middle, a small bar covered in golden accents and a few recliners that looked to be attached to the floor but spun a full three hundred and sixty degrees. "Follow me." Samual put his hand on her waist moving her gently to the side so he could move past her. She followed him to the back of the jet where there was a door. He turned the handle and extended an arm, motioning for her to enter first. There was a giant bed covered in feather pillows and the softest looking comforter she'd ever seen. "I assumed you were still tired, it's a long flight. We'll be out here if you need one of us." She smiled thanking him and let herself fall onto the down comforter. It wasn't long before she was back in a dreamless asleep.

Turbulence shook the plane enough to wake her from the deepest sleep she could ever remember getting. She rolled off the bed and went to join the guys in the main seating area. Zakarian was stretched out on one of the leather benches and Samual sat on the bench across from him sipping on an iced beverage reading through a magazine. She tapped Zakarian's shoulder to wake him up. "You can go sleep in the bed if you want, I've slept long enough." He stood up and walked straight to the bedroom without saying a word. He looked exhausted. She watched as he closed the door behind him.

"Good morning, gorgeous" She looked at Samual and saw he was now wearing a pair of black reading glasses. He looked so sophisticated and he had an adorable grin plastered to his face.

"Mmm, good morning to you as well, Sir." She stared at him and he was staring back at her. His eyes were dark, intense and she couldn't help but feel a tingle in her chest as she took him in. "How long do we have until we land?"

"Only a few hours. You've been sleeping for quite some time." He took a sip of his drink then motioned towards her head. "Is that a new look your trying?" She could tell he was holding back a laugh. She walked over to the restroom and looked in the mirror. She couldn't possibly look worse. Her makeup from the day before was smeared down her cheek and her naturally golden curls were a stunning replica of Medusa's. She cleaned up her face and ran her fingers through her hair trying to look as decent as she could, then pulled her hair back into a messy bun. She walked back out rubbing the sleep from her eyes still as she plopped down onto one of the rotating chairs. She rested her head on one of her hands and looked back at Samual. "Ah, much better. I mean, not that you didn't look good before." He commented, bringing a minor heat wave to her cheeks as she gave him a disbelieving look.

Samual wasn't sure what to think of Alveen. All he had seen of her since he got there was her confusion and disappointment, two things he was certain were not normal for her. He admired her from a distance for the time being. She had grown into a beautiful young woman. Aging was hard on anyone who was not from this world. Back on Beannaithe aging took them quite a bit longer. He was excited to get to know her more and discover what kind of woman she had become being so far from her culture. He watched her as she leaned against her hand in the spinning recliner. She was staring back at him only she wasn't embarrassed like he expected she would be from him pointing out her bed head. She just sat back, relaxed and he could feel her magic within her from where he sat. He could feel that she was strong, and he was going to show her how to pull all of that to the surface and use it correctly.

Samual went back to his reading that was provided on the jet and Alveen watched out the window. "So, how old are you?"

"Excuse me?" Samual answered, not expecting her to start conversation.

"Well.." She paused. "I've sat through many of my brothers lectures and if I'm not mistaken, elves, or at least in the sense that he teaches, are supposed to age very slowly, pretty much an immortal being, if they only died of old age. Zakarian is

* * *

going to be thirty this year, obviously he doesn't look that old, which I just figured was from great genetics. I obviously look my age... but how old are you?" He smiled at her rambling.

"In our world, I'm about two thousand five hundred and eighty years old. Which, in this world, would be impossible. But our world possesses magic that increases the length of lives and obviously, our eternal-like youth factor. Zakarian is about two thousand seven hundred if I'm not mistaken. You are much older than twenty, I'm afraid to tell you. With your age and birthday, you're about one thousand nine hundred and ninety years old? Approximately."

"Oh. That's great.. I feel like I got cheated out of life now" Alveen spoke sarcastically then continued. "Wait. If I'm really that old, how is it that I don't remember anything about this 'other world' I am supposedly a princess in?" he put his magazine down and looked directly into her eyes for a short second before speaking. He spoke in a very somber tone.

"You were injured. That was actually the reason you were sent away to be protected. One of the Syragons from the Dorcha tribe found you with your friends down by the lake near where you grew up. You were attacked, it was clear afterwards that their intent was to kill you. You suffered major trauma to your head and even with the magic we had at the time, there was no healing everything. You were healed physically but mentally, you forgot everything before that day, everything except Zakarian. He was the only one you would see or let near you. Everyone else was like strangers to you, including me." His facial expression didn't change but in those dark eyes, Alveen saw that her not remembering him, hurt him deeply. She couldn't help but wonder how close they had been. "Anyways, your grandmother decided it was best for you to be sent away, for the protection of you and the throne, especially since your father was still around as the next in line for the throne. Zakarian went with you being the only one you trusted at the time and being the other heir to the throne." He adjusted in his seat and his gaze was back to being concealed and happy. "And actually, you're still not old, you should probably look a little younger had you not come here. You did lose quite a bit of time being here but once we return the aging will slow. However, in our culture you are not old until you've reached about eight or nine thousand years old, which there are very few of. So, you and I still have quite a long time before we are considered old my dear." She sat back thinking for a moment.

"What is a syragon? I haven't heard Zakarian teach about them." She folded her arms and turned facing him, listening for the new knowledge she was hoping to get.

"They are an unnatural cross of a siren and dragon, able to live and breathe on land and under water. They are vicious, created by a sorceress, and unable to reproduce naturally. They look similar to a centaur, but much more disgusting and wild. With a rancid stench of.."

"Rotten seaweed and burning flesh?" she interrupted, the dreams replaying in her head as if she were there again. He looked at her shocked.

"How do you.?" he paused, almost looking hopeful, "Do you remember?"

"Sorry to disappoint but no. I've had very vivid dreams about them. I never knew what they were."

"Fascinating." He stared at her curious for what seemed like a long time. She turned and looked out the window, unsure of what to say or how much of that dream was real. Had that really been a memory, not a dream? How many of her dreams were her remembering her past life? It left her stomach in knots.

The plane finally landed and Zakarian emerged from the back room looking refreshed. Alveen looked out the window in awe at the boulders and flora that draped over the rolling hills she could see from the small airport they landed in.

"Alright, so we've got only a two-hour journey to the base of this mountain. Carrantuohill is the local name. This is actually the very first portal point we made here, and by far the strongest, making it safer for us to use on this particular occasion." Alveen pulled the straps of her backpack over her shoulders and followed Zakarian off the jet. At the bottom of the narrow staircase a small car waited for them. Samual was right, the journey only took a couple hours and there was remarkable terrain to see as they traveled. She had never been outside of where Zakarian had raised her, this was a whole new world for her.

The car slowed as Samual reached the trail that led to the mountain., putting it in park as the dirt road began to disappear. "We must walk from here" Samual stated bluntly as he crawled out of the vehicle. She followed along and they began the short hike toward the base of the tallest peak. The inclines were splashed with lavender and golden flowers that grew denser as the terrain grew closer to the two comparable bodies of water in the valley below. Alveen couldn't help but smile as she stared out on the horizon like it was a well-preserved priceless painting. "We made it!" Zakarian squatted down and picked up a shining green stone. From where Alveen stood it just looked like the grass was wet because it blended in so well. He picked it up and took a deep breath. "Everyone ready?"

"Um, what am I doing?" Alveen asked in an almost panicked voice.

"Just hold our hands. You're going to need both of us." Samual grabbed her hand tightly. "Don't let go." She looked back and forth between the two. Suddenly the wind swirled around them, her hair was tore from its tie and flew in all different directions. She looked at Zakarian and saw that his body was radiating white light. She quickly looked to Samual and saw his were doing the same. They both had their eyes closed and were taking deep breathes. She could see their lips moving but couldn't hear anything they were saying beyond the wind ripping around her. The beautiful colors around her were muted and above their heads was a large swirling pool. She was amazed and shocked. All this time she was thinking it was only mere fiction, but to see the portal with her own eyes made something inside her start to churn. She felt calm and light and powerful. She looked down and her hands were glowing with that same radiant white light. Samual looked down and his eyes widened, his lips still moving from whatever chant they were reciting. He squeezed her hand and smiled, reassuring her that everything was okay.

She took a few deep breathes and closed her eyes not sure of what to expect. The current of air finally grasped her. She felt her feet lift off the soft ground below her and the airstream forcing her body in different directions. The last coherent thought she had was that she was still holding someone's hand, then nothing.

~CHAPTER II~

WELCOME TO

BEANNAITHE

Zakarian felt the powerful wind enclose around his body as they were pulled through the portal and his body slammed into the rigid ground. Opening his eyes, he took in the tall grass surrounding him noticing he was in a clearing bordered by dense woods. As he collected his thoughts he focused on the familiar sense of less gravity than he had become accustomed to, the swaying of the plants in the warm breeze and the bold flora that accented the otherwise mud and grass landscaping. Quickly he stood to look for Alveen and Samual.

"She's unconscious." Zakarian turned at the sound of his friend's composed voice and saw Samual holding Alveen in his arms, sitting in the high meadow not far from where he now stood. He raced to her side, checking her pulse making sure she was indeed only unconscious.

"Only unconscious for now but we need a healer to look at her. Her body isn't accustomed to that sort of travel. I assume we are near home?" Samual nodded to him and carried her to their kingdom, Cosaint, where their grandmother and family friends resided. Most portals were in the center of kingdoms, so the receiving end could be guarded and monitored. This would become their home again.

"I'm taking her straight to The Queen, I'm sure she has many healers who we can trust to take care of her."

"I don't think we should leave her side."

"You stay with her first, we can take shifts." Samual suggested. Zakarian nodded in approval walking closely alongside him. "Here, you take her, I will run ahead to get a room prepared and a healer, I also need to inform The Queen of your arrival."

Zakarian took hold of Alveen in his arms as Samual sprinted towards the nearby town.

He wasted no effort to reach The Queen quickly. He doubted Zakarian was even close. He sped up the moss-covered ramp leading into the fortress of nature and jewels known as kingdoms palace. The time of day allowed streams of light to pour through the windows and open walls, illuminating the speckles of pollen as if glitter was part of the air itself. He looked up at the assistant standing outside The Queen's bed chambers, giving her a look that said he was in a hurry.

"Your Majesty." Samual insisted as he jogged into her bed chambers, announced by her assistant. It was bright, the furniture made of precious metals. She stood from her place in front of the fire in a simple chiffon gown. A single thick strap held the gown in place over her left shoulder, with a piece of fabric draping from it down her back like a thin cape. The lavender matched per peridot eyes impeccably. Her short black hair hung longer in the front framing her flawless features.

"Oh Samual, you have returned! What is the urgency?" She questioned with concern in her brow.

"Alveen; your granddaughter, She is unconscious from the portal travel. I would recommend having her rest in a healer's quarters until she awakens Zakarian insists on staying by her side."

"Yes right away. Leigheas is the best I've met in my time, she lives over across from the training grounds. Take her there. Please inform me when she wakes."

"Yes, Your Majesty." Samual bowed and headed back to the streets with haste where Zakarian would be. He approached and led him to Leigheas's quarters. After all, he was at the training grounds every day, so he knew exactly where he was going.

Leigheas must have been informed because the short brunette witch was at the bottom of an ivy covered staircase waiting for them. Without saying a word she led them to the room where Alveen would be watched over and pulled the silk blanket back from the oversized bed. Zakarian gently set her down and pulled the feather filled covers over her. "She has no injuries. She's just unconscious after a portal journey, nothing to worry about." Leigheas stated after her initial examination.

"Is that normal?" Zakarian spoke quickly.

"It will be alright my dear, she will be fine. She has only traveled one other time. Magic takes a toll on anyone who uses it. It is not something we see often since most of us have been conditioned for such exertion. We will keep an eye on her and within the next few hours, or days, she will wake. Some take longer than others." She gave a small curtsy and walked out of the room. After a few hours Samual decided he should get back to his normal routine.

A couple days had passed. Zakarian and Samual took turns staying in the room with her so she wasn't alone when she woke up. Samual was constantly stopping in during breaks while he was training since it wasn't a far trek.

"You think she'll be okay?"

"Yes, I promise you. Before we were pulled through, she touched her magic. She assisted us in getting back whether she was trying to or not. She's never used magic before. She's probably exhausted. Not to mention she's only traveled through a portal to a different world one other time, as Leigheas said." Samual was calming Zakarian down. Alveen had been unconscious for two days now since they arrived. He was worried sick about her and wouldn't leave her side, when he slept and Samual took watch he only moved to the next room over instead of returning to his room in the palace. Samual saw the glow from her that happened when elemental magic was being used. She hadn't drawn the magic out from herself, but she drew it from the elements around her when the wind swirled around them. "I'm going to get things organized for when she awakes. Let me know if she regains consciousness please." Zakarian smiled to his companion as he walked out and turned back to his sister.

"This is our home Alveen, where you really grew up. Where you had parents and you have a purpose. I promise you will love it." He whispered

"How can you promise something like that?" He watched in relief as her raspy voice escaped her smooth lips. His heart fluttered with excitement.

"I've been so worried about you." He pulled her in for a tight hug. "How are you feeling?" He guided her with his hands as she sat up. He motioned for a girl that was standing near the bedside to leave and go notify Samual.

"I'm feeling fine. What happened?" Alveen answered holding her head as if she were dizzy.

"We went through the portal."

"Seriously? I thought this was all just a dream." She leaned back against the headboard and tried to take in her surroundings noticing the vines and trees intertwined in such an elegant fashion making the walls and ceiling of the room they were in. "This place is magnificent." The floors were covered in moss and there was no door on the room, just a large opening in one of the walls.

"Samual said you touched your magic right before we were pulled through the portal." He stated quietly.

"I did?!" she felt excited, though she couldn't remember how she did it.

"I didn't see it, or feel it, but I guess he did."

"I do remember my hands glowing a little bit right before everything went black."

"Then as soon as you're feeling up to it I guess we will have to work on it." He looked for a reaction out of Alveen but she was still wrapping her head around everything. Just then Leigheas entered the room

"The Banri approaches." Through the opening in the tree trunk wall glided an athletic feminine figure with a thin emerald silk cloak draping off her shoulders and an ivory colored gown underneath it. As the woman came into the light her features were revealed to Alveen. She had silky black curls tucked back into a formal hair style with ringlets dancing to the sides of her peridot colored irises. Her skin was so pale she almost glowed in the dark and her thin lips a very light blush color. She had sharp features making her look very strong and proud, fierce even. Then she smiled. She looked to be in her fifty's but in pristine shape.

"Hello Alveen. I's so excited to have you home. I'm Vailion, your grandmother." She sat on the edge of the bed looking into Alveen's icey teal eyes. She reached up and twisted one of her granddaughter's blonde curls. "I can see your parents in you." She dropped the piece of hair and pulled her hand back.

"It's nice to meet another family member. I hope we can get time to reconnect."

"She is also the Banri of Cosaint." Alveen looked confused at Zakarian's comment. 'The Queen."

"Oh! Um, I apologize, I'm not sure what the proper way to greet a Queen is."

"Non-sense. You are recovering and unaware of our customs. When you are well, we will teach you our ways." Banri Vailion answered with a grin. "Normally a bow or curtsy will do as a greeting or farewell." She pointed out.

"She's awake?" She heard Samual's voice outside the wall and turned to see him. He walked in, now dressed in more casual attire wearing the same thin emerald cloak over his toned shoulders. She stared up at his powerful eyes as he approached the

• • •

bedside faster than expected. He wore that prefect smile like his favorite accessory. "Good morning Gorgeous." He said as he had on the plane.

"Do I really look that bad again?"

"No, not nearly as horrifying as you did before." She scoffed at him and he leaned down to give her a hug. "I'm happy to see you're awake and doing well. I have arranged your chambers, whenever you're ready someone will be available to take you there. I just wanted to stop in, but I need to get running to a training session. Which I hope she'll be joining soon?" He looked between Zakarian and Banri Vailion for approval.

"After we get her settled in and accustom to her new home, she is more than welcome to train if she wishes." The Banri told him.

"Then I'll see you soon Banphrionsa Alveen." Samual said and turned on his heels to leave.

"What did he just call me?"

"Banphrionsa. It's our equivalent to Princess." Zakarian explained. She felt flattered. She hadn't really thought about the fact that she was an actual Princess now. "Well we're going to let you rest. I'll be in the room next to you whenever you're ready to explore the village. You will need a new outfit." She looked down at her grass and dirt stained jeans and t-shirt she had changed into before they left their house.

It only took a couple hours for her to feel ready to move around. She stood, feeling the spongy moss under her bare feet. She glanced around to find her shoes with no luck. Voices were loud outside the entrance of the room, forcing her to follow her curiosity to the branch entwined railing that kept her from falling to the ground below. This world was like a fairytale. Everything was so vibrant and alive. She looked out in the distance to see a tall shimmering palace that the sun reflected off. There were mountains, waterfalls and creatures everywhere. She then looked around and observed people below until she came across a familiar face. Samual stood on the side of the field below looking up to her. He grinned happily at the sight of her and bowed holding eye contact. She blushed in return.

"Feeling better already?" Zakarian asked as Alveen tried to conceal her rosy cheeks.

"Much, I was just slightly dizzy. Didn't want to risk falling and further injuring myself." He didn't answer, "So what is going on here?" She nodded toward the field below where Samual stood.

"Ah, this is training. Every citizen of Cosaint, which is the kingdom you're in now and grew up in by the way, is trained to fight and be warriors. With the constant threat of the Dorcha Tribes we can't risk not having enough warriors at the ready."

"What is Samual doing down there?"

"That's his position. He is Head of the Palace Guard. He trains the new guards and sometimes, in his leisure time, he trains some of the novices."

"Impressive." She nodded. "He seems like a brilliant man." She paused noticing she may sound interested. She smiled brushing it off continuing the conversation.

"He is. He is highly respected, almost as respected as a pure blood. He has worked hard to get to his position." Maybe it wouldn't be too weird, Alveen thought, if she asked about how they were connected before, obviously he was familiar with her.

"I hope this doesn't strike you as odd, but how close were him and I before I was injured?" He looked at her surprised she even knew as much as she did. "We talked about it while you were sleeping on the flight. He seemed... hurt." He let out a deep sigh.

"You two were very close. You had an odd relationship from my point of view. At the time you were much younger than him and it seemed like he cared for you like a little sister." She wasn't sure how she felt about that. "He was actually the one who found you and carried you to the healers. You were playing with another young girl by the bay. You were constantly trying to talk to the mermaids." He laughed recollecting the memories.

"Mermaids? They exist too?"

"Oh yes. Mermaids, sirens, centaurs, elves obviously, fairies, witches. There are so many creatures that live in harmony here." He looked around, pointing to a different race if he saw one. "Anyways, he was practicing his training at his home, which happens to be near the bay, and heard a scream from where he was. He ran to your side and fought off the syragon that attacked you. Killed it in fact. Your friend didn't make it. He was still feeling guilty about it when we left." Alveen felt the hurt rushing into her. She lost a friend because a creature tried to kill her? "That event is actually what led to him being promoted. He saved The Princess and tried to save her friend. Not many face syragons and live to tell about it. And he is, even now, considered young. Deceitful, strong and evil creatures. They can travel by land and water but only in certain conditions. They live underwater though, in the abyss. Only on a double moon can they come on land and when they do, death follows. They try to find anyone who would potentially be a good candidate to transform into one of them. Fortunately, elves and all other magical creatures are not able. The magic in us fights the transformation, so it kills us instead of transforming us. When they come on land, much as a mermaid gains legs for a period of time, syragons gain half their body, like a centaur. They also have a gigantic set of wings. They are the ultimate deadly creature." Alveen stood there listening intently as she did during his lectures, with her arms crossed and her brow pushed together.

"They sound horrible." She whispered. "Samual killed one protecting me?"

"Yes. And please don't take this with offense, but I think his affection has always been more than that toward a little sister." Once again, he looked for a reaction as he handed her a cloak matching the one she had seen them wearing. "Might I suggest a stroll, Your Highness?" He held his arm out for Alveen to take so he could walk her down the staircase after she wrapped the cloak around her and pulled up the hood to cover her poorly maintained hair. "We need to get you an outfit fit for a Banphrionsa!" Alveen smiled excitedly at the thought of new clothes.

"Shall we?" She said walking arm in arm with her brother. "So, what is the proper apparel wore here?"

"Think comfort and flexibility. You will see a lot of women who wear skirts with tall slits up each leg, it allows them to move and to fight if the time came. Many wear flexible materials that stretch with their bodies for the same reason. We do have similar materials you're use to here as well, those are considered more restricting but many times they are wore during riding to protect the inner legs."

"Riding what exactly?"

"Alicorns. It's like our version of horses. Only they have the horn of a unicorn and feathered wings like Pegasus. They are trustworthy creatures and the ability to run and fly is extremely useful. You have one. I will have to reintroduce you to him. His name is Allicent."

They walked through the streets and Zakarian told her of some of the families that lived in which houses and where all the shops were that she would enjoy and tried to teach her about the history, but Alveen was fascinated by the glimmering beauty of what Zakarian had called a village. Gemstones lined everything, and the most amazing part was everything was made from nature, literally. Apparently, the architects in this world were sorcerers of many kinds that used their magic and studies to manipulate the growth of trees, branches, vines, flowers, moss and any other natural life to create the homes and stores that lined the streets. In some areas there was very little sun shining through due to the thick canopy of leaves above. The streets were completely made of stepping stones, with moss growing between them. It was truly enchanting.

~CHAPTER III~

THE MOST DIVINE

Alveen's eyes widened when she saw they were approaching the radiant palace that she saw from the railing. "What is this place?"

"This is your home. The Cosaint Palace, where the royals live and conduct business." She squeezed his arm in excitement as they walked up the moss blanketed ramp.

"We will go to your chamber first to find you an outfit before we flaunt you around the palace. Maybe we will do something with that mess of curls on your head as well." She scoffed pretending to be offended but she could only imagine how glamorous her hair looked yet again. They walked through tall hallways lined with pointed archways intertwined with what she would describe as celtic designs. The intricate detail in every corner of the huge palace was second to none. From the outside it looked as if it were made of diamonds shimmering in the sunlight, but when you crossed the threshold it was as if you entered an ancient ruin, being held together by the sunlight itself. Zakarian reached for a set of double french styled wooden doors after they had wandered through the maze of corridors, hesitated for suspense and pushed the doors open to Alveen's room, which she remembered Samual had instructed be made up for her.

The floor was covered in that same soft moss that was in the healer's home, on the far end of the room was a large open balcony that looked down over a glittering body of water where she could see the alicorns that Zakarian spoke of flying high into the rays of sunlight. Her bed was in a tall posted bed frame made completely of driftwood, accented and held together with strands of pure silver with the same pillows and blankets that the jet had. She wondered where they came from. Opposite the room from the bed was a large vanity made of driftwood and silver to match her bed frame. She investigated the mirror and ran her fingers over the back of the chair that sat in front of it. She was still in the outfit that she wore through the portal. Her fitted blue jeans were rolled up so they ended below her mid shin, and she wore a black v neck t-shirt that hugged her curves. They gave her one of the thin emerald cloaks to wear around, so her attire wasn't as noticeable, even though she wouldn't have stood out much. She looked down noticing she was still barefoot. Looking in the mirror she admired herself for a moment, her golden curls brushed the center of her shoulder blades and her eyes shined a brilliant shade of teal. "It's beautiful." She continued to admire the room.

"I'm going to inform grandmother that you are dressing, I will be back in a couple hours to retrieve you and we can have lunch with her." He started towards the door, "Your finest clothing is in the closet over here" he pointed towards a glass door on one side of the room and walked out.

She ran over to the closet, excited to change clothes finally. When she pulled the door open, she was overwhelmed with gowns of the finest cut. Jewels adorned the bodices, beading and embroidery hugged the details on every dress. They had to be more expensive than anything she'd ever owned before. As she was walking through the open closet she saw one dress was hanging up all alone on the back wall. It was a mesmerizing shade of blue, maybe green? The way the light hit it made it changes colors. It was a dropped waist, strapless, light weight gown with a glittering fabric that flowed down the bodice and draped along the skirt. The top had a V shaped neckline that came to a point at each of her shoulders. Along with it was a set of blue fire opal jewelry and a dark emerald hooded cloak with beading sporadically sewn on. It was obvious this was what she was supposed to wear.

A young girl entered the room and showed her where to shower and clean up. She was grateful to see they had running water and it wasn't terribly different than what she was used to. By the medieval theme that encompassed this world she had begun to feel nervous about basic amenities. She also discovered though they didn't have electricity, the magic more than sufficed for lighting. Alveen walked out of the bathroom and the girl was still there. "Oh, I apologize, I didn't mean to keep you. What can I do for you?" She asked the girl.

"Your Highness, I'm here to help you." She laughed quietly. "I can help you tie your gown and possibly do your hair if you wish?" She was very sweet and Alveen admitted she did need help with her uncontrollable curls.

"Of course, let me get the gown on and then I will be out." Alveen quickly crawled into the dress through the bottom and let it fall over her curves, letting her hips catch it. The girl walked in and tied the bodice tightly.

"You look so beautiful, Your Highness." Alveen was still not use to the title.

"I've never felt this beautiful before." She admired the fit of the gorgeous gown and how the color made her eyes brighten.

"Just wait until we do your hair." The girl exclaimed excited. After the jewelry was put on, the girl worked on Alveen's curls. She was gentle, twisting her strands of hair and pinning them into place. When she was done, Alveen opened her eyes and saw her spiraled locks twisted perfectly into a high formal updo, minus one strand that caressed her cheek. "Now for the final touch." The girl went to the closet and brought a box to Alveen. "You pick which one you wish to wear." The box was lined with velvet and held at least a dozen crowns. One was the same silver color that adorned the emerald cloak and was twisted into the shape of vines and leaves with those same blue fire opals set in place. It didn't stand tall, but it was the perfect accessory for a Princess. "Are you ready?"

"I hope so. How do I look?"

"You look stunning. Be confident Your Highness." This made Alveen smile brightly. Then a knock came at the door.

"Are you ready sister?"

"Yes, come in." She stood up and faced the door, slowly walking towards it waiting to see her brother enter. He looked dashing in a nice suit as usual. His hair stylishly combed and tied at the nape of his neck and he had made sure to shave, leaving the scent of aftershave swarming him. She waited for his reaction.

"Holy.." he paused taking her in for a moment. "Where did my little sister go?" he gave her a hug and spun her around. "Where did that gown come from, it's simply divine!"

"It was in my closet." He gave a curious look.

"Well, it looks as if it was made for you." He held a box in his hand and handed it to her. "Here these are for you." She pulled the cover back and stared down onto a sparkly pair of silver flats lined with white leaves and clear gemstones. She set them on the ground and slid her foot in, feeling like Cinderella when they fit perfectly. "Now you are ready." Zakarian smiled and led her to the dining hall. Everyone bowed or curtsied as she walked by and it only made her feel awkward. Zakarian couldn't help but laugh yet admire her innocence and kindness in regarding her subjects. The royals were never cruel to their people, but they knew there was a distinct line of respect to be followed.

● ● ●

"Is that my granddaughter I see!?" Banri Vailion's voice echoed through the tall trees that made up the dining hall. "My, my, you are truly the most beautiful Princess I've ever laid eyes on." She looked her over. "That gown is exquisite, one of the finest. Where did you find it?"

"It was in my closet, thank-you so much. I've never felt this beautiful before." They spoke over a meal of exquisitely seasoned vegetables that she didn't recognize. The Banri asked of the things Alveen enjoyed back on Inaitithe, which was the local name for what she had known as Earth. The dinner didn't last long before The Banri was called to a meeting. They said their farewells and Alveen parted ways with Zakarian, deciding to explore the village further.

~CHAPTER IV~

MATTERS OF THE HEART

The streets were full of life, even as the sun was setting over the horizon. Music played and Alveen couldn't help but let herself smile. As she walked down the street, faces lit up with joy and everyone bowed as she passed them. She even danced with some of the young creatures in the village and introduced herself to a few of the parents. Attention was never something Alveen needed much of but it was nice to be noticed and for her subjects to be excited to see her.

* * *

She continued down the wide pebbled path towards the training grounds in hope of finding Samual. As she approached the grounds her heart fluttered and she felt the need to look her absolute best, as if the dress and her hair weren't already doing her wonders. She straightened her posture and stood tall, clasping her hands together in front of her as she strolled forward.

The training grounds were empty. She crossed her arms, curious. A strong breeze entered the grounds forcing her to pull her velvet emerald cloak closed around her to keep the chill out. It carried flowers and leaves making it easy for her to determine the direction. The wind spiraled over the center of the field in front of her and that familiar white radiant light glowed dimly from the center. One by one elves, centaurs, witches and fairies emerged from what she now recognized as the receiving end of a portal. Lastly, Samual jogged out from the center of the portal dismissing his group of trainees. The breeze dispersed, and she released the hold on her cloak, revealing the exquisite fabrics of the dress underneath.

"Is this what you do all day? Just travel to different worlds and play around?" Samual turned at the sound of her voice and his expression reflected his joy to see her.

"I knew that dress would look ravishing on you." He turned and slowly walked towards her, his eyes approving of her attire. "Do you like it?"

"You are the one who put this in my closet?" She questioned shocked.

"Of course. I prepared your room, I personally had this made for you over the last few days." He continued to look her over, folding his arms and rested his chin on his hand. "I'm not sure how I feel about the new hair style though." Leaving her to wonder what exactly he meant by it.

"Why? Is it wild and untamed again? I swore this would hold for days." She exclaimed reaching for her pins. Before she could adjust the first one, Samual's hands reached up and stopped her.

"Not at all. It's perfect. Too perfect." He looked down at his boots as he stepped even closer towards her, as if he was embarrassed by what he would say next, "It's the wild and untamed hair that I like." As close as he was to her she had no choice but to look him over. She admired the rough stubble that had grown out in the last couple days, though it still showed off his masculine jaw line. She had never been flirted with before and she had no idea how to respond to it. Her chest tightened thinking of the words he just spoke to her.

He was looking down into her eyes. They were sparkling in the little bit of sunlight that was left from the day. He hated how easily they trapped him and held his attention. The beautiful, rare shade that they reminded him of the sea. A bright teal color that changed from blue to green depending on her mood, they were unique in the way they were rimmed with a golden hue. He remembered when they were younger, every time she would cry her eyes would turn into the peridot green that her grandmothers were. She batted her eyelashes unknowingly making his chest tighten with nerves.

"So where are you off too now?" She asked to break the silence. Samual snapped out of the trance she had him in and stood tall, backing away so she wouldn't realize his lack of control.

"I have no plans, I was actually going to come see how you were doing."

"Really?" His flattery won her over. "Well. I am doing well." They stood there silent for a few moments. It had never been like this when they spoke before, like they were both nervous school children.

"Would you be interested in spending the rest of the day with me?" he suggested.

"That sounds delightful." She reached for the crook of his arm and let him lead her towards the woods. The stone pathway continued through, so it must have been a well-known trail, she thought to herself. Alveen wanted to bring up what Zakarian had said. How did Samual view her? The more time she spent with him the more convinced she was that he had feelings for her, as Zakarian had put it, more than just those one holds for a sibling. Zakarian and Samual had been the best of friends, surely Samual would have said something to him if he had grown feelings for his best friend's younger sister. They walked for a short period of time before Samual broke the silence.

"How are you enjoying Cosaint so far?"

"It's lovely. I haven't had much time to explore like I wished yet. It seems grandmother has me on a rather short leash until I learn the appropriate customs and ways of this culture."

"You like exploring?" he would not have guessed that about her. She seemed like a girl that stayed to herself and not one to wander.

"I love little adventures." She clarified, "Discovering new things is one of my many passions. Although this discovery was quite unexpected." Glancing around she noticed the cathedral height of the trees and it was getting rather dark. "Should we be turning back by now?" she became nervous. This was a world she was not familiar with, and from what she had learned thus far, the dark held very real monsters.

"You have nothing to fear." He reached his hand across and squeezed one of hers that was gripping onto his bicep as if she feared he would leave her alone. "Do you trust me?" he asked, stopping and taking her chin in his hand making her look into his eyes, those eyes that she always found herself getting lost in, even before she realized the attraction.

"I'm not entirely sure yet." He looked disappointed with her answer. Dropping his arm, he turned and faced her when he spoke.

"I am no one to fear, Banphrionsa. I have protected your family, and you, for many years. Allow me to show you." Butterflies danced in her stomach when he called her Princess in their native language. She wanted to trust him, and she knew he could show her this world and teach her so much, but all she felt right now was nervous and scared as the sunlight continued to leave the sky. She remembered how Zakarian spoke of him and how he protected her from a very real deadly situation. Zakarian trusted him, so she could too, right? "Hold my arm." He held out his bent elbow again waiting for her gentle touch. She looped one arm through it and rested her other hand on his upper arm again as if she didn't want to part with him. "Close your eyes." She looked up skeptically at him then closed her eyes and walked with him.

It was a short walk before he pulled her down onto what felt like a log that they sat on. She kept her eyes closed until he said otherwise. "Can I open them yet?"

"Wait here one second" he felt her grip tighten around his arm "I promise I won't leave you Alveen. Trust me." Her grip relaxed and she placed her folded hands in her lap, waiting for him to return. She heard his footsteps rustle through the foliage nearby and walk back directly in front of her. "Open your eyes." Her black vision gave way to an extraordinary display of bioluminescence. White, blue, green, pinks, oranges and yellows all contrasting the dark background the world provided at night. Fairies flew through the heights of trees like shooting stars back on Initithe. Flowers, leaves, vines and rocks glowed in the darkness, making the dark seem anything but terrifying. Samual stood in front of her with his hand reaching down, offering to help her stand up. "What do you think?"

"How did you do this?" she questioned in awe still allowing her gaze to explore the anomaly before her.

"It's a natural occurrence. Many creatures have the ability, even living plant life has the ability. It is all in the magic of the world. Your old world possessed much of this magic, but very few creatures even knew how to extract it." He pulled a bouquet of flowers out from behind his back. Blues and greens, just like her dress, the roots all tangled together with soil around them and a large leaf holding it all together. "These are for you." He handed them to her. "I hope you like them. They are held together so you can plant them somewhere else and they will continue to live" Even in his sensitive moments, Alveen noticed he still appeared very strong and in charge. He was not the kind of nervous she had witnessed in school scenarios, he was attentive and straight forward. He was hopeful and understanding with her.

"I do love them." Standing up on her toes she placed a gentle kiss on his cheek. She saw the surprise on his face by the glow of her flowers. Alveen smiled, appreciative of the admiration that Samual showed. "Can I ask you something?"

"Anything."

"Zakarian said you and I were very close before.." she hesitated hoping this was the right time. "before I was injured. He also told me you were the one who saved me."

"Both of those statements are true. So, what is your question?"

"I'm not sure. I guess I was just hoping you could tell me more about our connection before I forgot everything." He didn't answer. "I saw the hurt in your eyes on the plane. I know there is more."

"It seems so irrelevant now." he chuckled and let out a deep breath, which was something he did right before he spoke seriously on numerous occasions to her. "You were very young, though not in your old world's standards. You were still in the academy to learn your duties as Banphrionsa, I had been out of training and was starting my years in the Palace Guard, though I didn't obtain a higher station until your injury. I grew feelings for you. I spoke to Zakarian about it and I believed they were feelings an older brother would feel for his sister." He wasn't looking at her anymore. "Yes, I was hurt when you didn't remember me because I had been the one who was by your side nearly every day. I was the one who escorted you around town while Zakarian was off dealing with his princely duties. Not that he neglected you by any means, I was simply around more. And he was the one you remembered. I suppose part of me was jealous, though at the time I didn't realize why." He chuckled under his breath and stood up running his hands through the stylish mess on his head. "And it wasn't until I saw you again that I really realized what I felt for you." His hands were connected behind his back, his shoulders pushed back like he was a solider talking to a superior. His jaw line was tense, and she found herself attracted to him even more. "You were beautiful, but I did not have the rank or respect to even consider pursuing you as more than a friend. Then I was sent to find you." He paused meeting her eyes, for the first time, not looking entirely in control of his emotions. "And our circumstances have changed." He paused realizing what he unintentionally told her.

"You knew me as a young girl. You have not known me as the young woman, so far from her culture, that I am now."

"I understand. That is why I have not brought it up. I wanted you to seek me and for it to be by your choosing that.." he trailed off unable to find the next words to speak to her. His heart was full when she was around. Even in the short time they had spent together since he found them, he admired every little thing about her. Her laugh that made her eyes sparkle, the way she was confident and intelligent. He sat back and listened to the conversations her and Zakarian held and her mind was so full of wonder and she was not that much different in heart than she was before. Alveen heard the pain his rough vocals carried as he spoke. She had never had someone who wanted more than a friendship with her, and she didn't know how to react. He sat on the glowing log next to her resting his elbows on his knees, clasping his hands together. He was frustrated and Alveen noticed that admitting his emotions was tremendously difficult for him. She could feel his hurt even when he was composed, as he was on the plane. Maybe, she thought, that's how it was before.

"I do wish to spend more time with you Samual. You are charming and respectful. I understand your frustration and I wish I could ease it." She wanted to give him hope that maybe someday soon there would be more between them, but she wasn't certain on her feelings for him yet or her place here and giving false hope was the last thing she wanted to do to the honest, caring man before her. Samual slouched down to the forest floor, resting against the log Alveen sat on. He leaned back and his eyes glimmered as he looked up to Alveen's face. He couldn't help but smile when he looked at her, "What was I like?"

He closed his eyes and his smile broadened as he thought about the younger version of her. "Much like you are now, only much more opinionated and outspoken." He laughed at the last part.

"I don't believe that."

"No, truly you were." He scanned the forest floor as if he would find answers there. "You didn't let anyone put you down or think they could get away with being rude to you. You were not cruel by any means, but you were forthright. Especially to me."

"I was rude to you? And you still had feelings for me?"

"Not rude, but you could see right through me. If anything bothered me, somehow you always knew. And you always confronted me about it and were very persistent, convinced that you could help fix whatever it was."

"And?"

"And.." he got to his feet holding his elbow out once again for them to head back into the palace. "You always did." A bashful smile played across his lips. She reached for his upper arm again, holding her flowers in the other.

"Thank-you." Alveen whispered deciding not much talk was needed on this walk back. "This was spectacular." He leaned down and brought her hand to his lips.

"Anything for you, Banphrionsa." Her palms started sweating and she bit her bottom lip nervously. She leaned against his arm as they walked. She could have guessed it from his slim fitting suit he wore when they first met, but underneath that thin shirt that he now wore, she felt a toned bicep as evidence of his years of training.

"Here you are, Banphrionsa Alveen." They stood at the door of her room within the palace.

"You didn't have to escort me all the way back here."

"Actually I did, I would have been neglecting my duties as Head of the Palace Guard to allow you to walk home alone at such a late hour."

"Oh." She said feeling foolish that she had thought he was being chivalrous.

"But I would have done so either way. For my own sake, so I knew you were safe." He corrected himself after he noticed she thought he was being a gentleman out of duty, not from his heart.

"I understand." She wasn't upset, she was amused at his nervous banter. "Will I be seeing you tomorrow?"

"I'm afraid not. The Banri has a tight schedule for you over the next couple of weeks." He tried to hide his disappointment, but she saw right through it. "But I will try to visit when time allows. I do need to attend to my training."

"Where do you live?" the thought of him walking alone left her restless, not that he couldn't take care of himself.

"Down by the bay. You can actually see my home from your balcony." Samual answered flirtatiously as if hinting towards her spying on him. His rough exterior was back and Alveen was coming to enjoy both his playful and protective side. She looked up into his passionate dark eyes. He was most certainly a beautiful man. His barley grown out facial hair gave him a very seductive look. She admired his facial features for a moment more before he bowed. He stood tall and leaned in towards her ear. "Sweet dreams Princess." He whispered so close she could smell his warm minty breath that skimmed across the skin of her neck.

"To you as well." She whispered back. He walked off with an enticing smile glued to his face.

~CHAPTER V~

THE COURSE OF NATURE

The moonlight lit up everything in her room through her balcony, leaving her no need for a light. First the flowers needed to go in a vase until she had time to plant them. Searching for a container she emptied one from the bathroom, filled it with the dirt inside the leaf and gently set her bioluminescent floral arrangement in the glass container.

Hanging up her dress she admired it one last time before she placed the jewelry and crown back in their secure locations. She pulled a soft t-shirt over her head and wiggled into a pair of dark green spandex pants. Sitting in front of the mirror she hunted for all the pins the girl had put in her hair earlier.

• • •

Alveen's wild curls flowed over her shoulder once again and she left a pile of pins sitting on her vanity table. The night's warm breeze slithered in through the open doors, drawing her out to the balcony. The bay below glistened in the moonlight.

A light turned on in trees below, illuminating what looked like a tree house. She squinted to see what was going on. An emerald cloak hung on the railing of the home. A smile found her lips when she saw his familiar figure. Samual had made it home safely and was right, she could see his home from her room. She felt like she was invading his privacy. The sound of her door opening made her spin around. Zakarian was walking in, his hand glowing to light the way.

"Ah, you have returned! How was the village?"

"It was enjoyable." He saw the flowers on her desk glowing in the darkness and gave her a look of curiosity, "I got them while I was out. Beautiful, aren't they? I've never seen anything like them." She wasn't ready to tell Zakarian about Samual, since she wasn't entirely sure what there was between them.

"Exquisite, I agree. Are you ready for your courses to start tomorrow?"

"Yes, of course." Her voice was low.

"Is something bothering you sister?" Zakarian questioned, nonchalantly sending the magical glowing orb that rested in his hand to the fixture in her vanity, lighting up the room enough for them to clearly see each other. He wore another finely tailored suit. Elegance seemed to be the dress code here. Gowns were only for royals, suits were formal attire as she was used to, and she saw many people in comfortable pants such as the material she used to wear.

"Not at all. I'm a little nervous for learning my place here. I don't want to disrupt any kind of balance that was made in my absence."

"You have nothing to worry about." He reassured her as she walked back into her room closing the large doors to her balcony and falling onto her oversized bed. "You will have private tutors that will be teaching you the basics and everything you need to know. They are not to waste their time on nonsense so try to obtain as much as you can."

"I've always been a good student. I'm not worried about the lessons." Alveen sat up in her bed and crawled under the covers leaning back against her silver entwined headboard.

"I'm aware. I'm just trying to prep you."

"When am I allowed to start doing magic?"

Zakarian chuckled, "After you learn the rules. Magic is costly if used improperly, but," he paused, muttering under his breath, holding his hand out in front of him then he blew on his palms and what looked like black glitter gently floated above them. The ceiling turned into the night sky, she laid back in her bed as if it were in the middle of a field and she could fall asleep under the stars. "incredible if done right. Maybe I will help you access it little by little. You must learn the language of this world though. Similar to how back on Initithe, they trained certain dog breeds with their origin language; that is the only way you can control the magic here."

Alveen nodded in understanding but started to drift off. "I will see you tomorrow then?"

"I will walk you to your first class." He walked out of the room, stealing the light and holding it in his palm once more. She rolled over on her side and looked out the glass doors thinking about how Samual wasn't far away at all, and how it was probably a good thing Zakarian came in when he did, for she was feeling guilty looking down on Samual's home without his knowledge. She drifted off into a deep sleep.

The morning came quickly with the rays of sun shining through the glass doors, illuminating the particles that twirled in the air. Alveen tossed the light weight covers off her so she could stand up and stretch for a few minutes before she prepared for her day. She stretched her thighs, arms and back and yawned multiple times as she walked over to the gown filled closet. She dragged her hand over the teal gown that Samual had custom made for her, smiling at the beauty.

She sifted through the gowns, each one more beautiful than the last. Since it was just courses she was doing today she parted the hangers and looked over a dark grey taffeta like gown that rested at her natural waist. It had elbow length sleeves that sat off her shoulders with hunter green embroidery down the skirt and wrapping the bodice. Pulling it off the hanger she changed quickly, then scavenged through the drawers to find matching jewelry and a tiara. She settled on a pair of simple emerald earrings and a matching teardrop emerald necklace.

"Your Highness" The young girl curtsied as Alveen walked out of the bathroom. "Your hair?" She inquired.

"Yes please, can we possible do something simple and casual?"

"Yes, Your Highness." The young girl's fingers were fast as she pulled strands of hair apart and began twisting them together off to one side in a braid. The tiara was slid between her curls and the young girl stepped back admiring her work. Alveen looked herself over in the mirror, smiling in approval.

"Thank-you very much" a knock on the door came only a second after, and in walked Zakarian.

"I'm here to escort you to your courses." He stated bluntly. He looked well rested. "First is History."

"Oh, lovely! I've always enjoyed history. Though I'm sure I will know nothing of the history here." They locked arms and walked through the vine covered halls to the other side of the palace entering the library, where an older gentleman sat. The room was even more detailed than the dining hall. Branches twisted into shelves for the walls of books, gold filigree danced into the crevices of the leaves and twigs, brightening the room. At the end of the room where the gentleman sat was an oversized fireplace, her head only just coming to the top of the mantel. Each of side of the detailed fireplace held giant arched windows that warmed the room with the sunlight beaming through. She continued to admire the railings and details as Zakarian spoke.

"This is Ollamh Hilfyro. He will be your tutor for most of your courses. He is a wise and patient teacher." Zakarian bowed to him as they approached. The man looked to be in his fifties, which she couldn't imagine how old that was here. He has silver hair tied at the base of his neck, keeping the shoulder length strands in place. His eyes were a mix of gold and green and his features were what she would call friendly and happy. He looked genuine.

"Ah! Banphrionsa, it's so wonderful to finally meet you." He bowed to her and held his hand out to lead her to her chair. Zakarian stayed for a short while to make sure all was going well. "You can simply call me Hilfyro, are we ready to begin?" She nodded her head and sat back in the velvet upholstered chair, surprisingly like the ones they use to have in their dining room. "Very good. Now I will be teaching you the basics; History, Science and Language. All three which are extremely different from what you are used to. Anything extra, such as magic control, sword fighting, nature manipulation, anything along those subjects, will be taught by others, though I am quite good at the first and last." He handed Alveen a couple large books and went over the basics of them with her. Zakarian leaned against the wall watching her. He saw an old friend from the corner of his eye.

"I will be back periodically to check on you, please pay attention Alveen." He walked off before she could protest. As he rounded the corner he saw a woman he remembered all too well leaning against the wall as if she was waiting for him. Long straight black hair flowed around her hips, cute smooth features, eyes the rarest shade of pink and the figure of a talented swimmer. She glowed the way fairies do when they are filled with joy. "How long has it been?" He walked towards her, smile broadening with every step.

"I've missed you." She threw herself in his arms and he held her. Malika was his long-time partner, romantically. They had been in love since they were little and never grew apart. It had been a frowned upon relationship since she had no elf in her at all, only mermaid and fairy.

"I have missed you more." He paused taking in her beauty, "How has everything been?" She seemed troubled.

"Do you have time to speak with me?"

"I always have time for you Malika." Holding hands they walked down the corridor talking of everything that he had missed since he left and how she was one of the female trainers now in the guard. They stopped at a large door, which Zakarian knew to be the youth care center. "What are we doing here?" Her gaze went to the floor and she struggled to keep a straight face.

"I want you to meet someone." Zakarian was momentarily confused. She pushed the doors open and they scanned the room of young creatures, until one of them stuck out to him. A young girl with those same pale pink eyes, only she bore features of an elf. Her cheek bones and jaw line were sharp like a warrior that possessed complete confidence. He was baffled. "Tanilly, come here." The young girl pranced over to her mother, staring at Zakarian. "This is Zakarian, he's going to hang out with us today." They went to a nearby restaurant with a playground area for Tanilly.

"Who's is she?" He questioned after the girl ran off to play. He was hurt that the love of his life could possibly have found another and started a family, and she never mentioned anything about this while they were talking.

"She's yours." Zakarian stood in shock. Was that even possible? "Right before you left it must have happened. I didn't even know until after you had gone already."

"You have been raising her on your own?" she shook her head in confirmation. "Does anyone else know about this, that I'm a father?" she shook her head acknowledging that no one did. He wasn't quite sure what to do. "She's beautiful."

"She takes after her father." Malika reached for Zakarian's hand. "She is so much like you. She is smart and so much fun. And she is even a bit mischievous."

"That sounds nothing like me." He laughed sarcastically. "So, what would you like me to do about this?"

"Well.." she trailed off and looked back at her daughter hopping from tree stump to tree stump, "I was hoping you would considering raising her with me. We could be a family."

"I would want nothing more my love, but I do need to address this in the palace before any official decision can be made. With her not being full elf, she may not be considered royalty and with my grandmother being so against our relationship in the beginning, I'm not sure how things will turn out."

"I understand. Will you at least spend time with her, as a companion of mine?"

"Most certainly." Zakarian squeezed her hand quick sending her a loving glance. He sat and wondered how he was going to tell his grandmother, or Alveen. Alveen wouldn't mind as much but she would not understand the delicacy of the situation. Maybe Samual would be able to help, he seemed to have been able to get very close to Alveen and explain things better.

Back in the library, Alveen sat intrigued by the history of the land and enjoyed learning the maps immensely. She had never seen such bizarre terrain before and everything was foreign to her. She learned of other kingdoms. Going over the map she realized this world, though it held so much more than Earth ever did, it was immensely smaller in size.

"This here is where the Dorcha tribes reside." Hilfyro explained as his lean arm stretched across the faded map they studied. "or more commonly known as 'The Darklands". Alveen remembered Zakarian talk a little bit about the Dorcha tribes, but she didn't know much.

"Who exactly are the Dorcha tribes? Why are they bad? I've heard people mention them, but I don't quite know the story" Alveen questioned. She leaned back in her chair like she knew it was going to be a long and fascinating story.

"They are us, only they have broken off from our community because they don't like elves being in charge, the sorceresses think they should be at the top of our hierarchy, and they do not follow any rules or guidelines with magic." He looked appalled talking about them. "Magic is fragile and the moment you use it for something outside the guidelines for which it was given to us, the balance is disrupted, for example, syragons."

"The sorceress created them." She interrupted, excited that she knew something.

"Correct. Well. All the original sorceresses and sorcerers came together. There were ten of them total. They believed in creating a creature with no soul, no emotion, a weapon essentially.

We knew about the plan only shortly before it was executed, but your great, great grandfather and grandmother arrived there just as the first litter was created. He destroyed the object being used to create them, killing four of the sorceresses in the process. Your great, great grandmother placed a curse on the litter that was already made, they were banished to the darkest abyss of our seas, but unfortunately it couldn't always be that way. Since it was on a double moon when the magic was performed, that was the night they were on land, and were released from their curse every double moon, which around here only occurs every two millennia, the last three double moons we haven't had any attacks or heard of their moving, aside from your attack of course."

Alveen watched the professor's eyes as he told the story as if remembering something at the same time. "What happened to the rest of the sorcerers?"

"Three more of them died in the battle that evening. Since then two have lost their lives to other quarrels aside from ours. One remains; the final sorceress. She is said to be the most vial of them all. She summons the syragons every double moon to do her bidding, though she has many more minions."

"So what keeps her from doing anything to us right now? I mean she sounds like she doesn't need syragons to end us." She said hopelessly.

"Ah, but everyone in the Solas tribes, living on the mountains, has magic. We are closer to our magic source than they are. Many of her minions are not able to perform magic, which is good and bad for her. With them not being able to perform or summon magic, they are the perfect candidates for a syragon transformation, or making of a syragon."

"That sounds terrible."

"Yes, it is quite horrifying when you get into the details, but back to the history. Our lands were separated many generations ago. A barrier was put up around our tribes, to protect us, though it doesn't always work. We have concluded that when an elder of the elves passes on, one that helped place the barrier, the wall falls until it is replaced. Any Dorcha inside when it goes back up are stuck inside with all of us, which generally doesn't end well for them."

"So, it was like an on-going whole world war?"

"I guess you could call it that, yes." They continued with their session for a short while longer until they were interrupted by Banri Vailion.

~Chapter VI~

No Mother of mine

"How are your studies coming along?" The Banri spoke with a sweet tone Alveen had not heard before.

"Wonderful, I am learning so much and it is all so fascinating." Alveen answered as she bowed slightly flicking her silver gown.

"I am glad to hear this. Hilfyro, you wouldn't mind if I stole my granddaughter away for a little while, would you?"

"Of course not, Your Majesty." He bowed and walked out of the library. Alveen's eyes flowed over her grandmother's red velvet, long sleeved gown with a gold embroidered belt and neckline, as if looking for imperfections. She walked away in the direction of a window. Alveen assumed she was to follow.

"My dear." Banri Vailion gestured towards a seat adjacent herself in front of a large open window.

"How are you today grandmother?"

"Splendid darling." She paused and looked into her granddaughter's eyes letting out a sigh. "I'm not one for much small talk, I'm sorry. Do you know where your brother is?"

"I'm not sure, he said he would check on me, so I would think he would be back sometime soon."

"Perfect, I need to speak with the two of you, when he arrives, bring him to the throne room. I need you and him to be aware of certain things and I would rather you hear it all from me."

"Yes, Your Majesty. We will meet you as soon as he returns." The Banri glided out of the library. Alveen sat back in her chair wondering what could be so important that she pulled her out of her studies and needs Zakarian as well.

It was only minutes before Zakarian walked in the door. "Where's Hilfyro?"

"Grandmother wishes to see both of us in the throne room. Now."

"Any idea what for?" Zakarian became nervous wondering if his grandmother had found out his secret.

"Not a clue." Zakarian and Alveen walked harmoniously to the throne room, Alveen waving to the guards as they entered, receiving a bow in return. They stepped up to the base of the throne and bowed waiting for The Banri to speak.

"So nice to see you both."

"As well as you grandmother. It's my understanding you have news to share with us?" Zakarian spoke as if he was in a hurry.

"Yes." She stood up and let out a long deep breath, allowing one of her curls to fall loose of her tightly bound hair but not giving it any attention. "We have reason to believe your mother is still alive and working within the Dorcha tribes."

"What? No. She would never do that." Zakarian defended without giving the news a thought.

"We have scouts that have reported seeing her. They are still only suspicions, but I thought it wise to not keep this information from you."

"Do we have any reason to believe she could have been kidnapped?" Alveen asked wondering what the real story behind this was.

"No, not that we are aware of. We have had no signs of her until our scouts brought it to our attention." She sighed stepping towards them, "I would not normally relay this type of information with such little evidence, but I wanted you both to be mentally prepared, should the day come that you have to face her."

"If it is indeed her, what do you think her purpose would be? What would have made her abandon her kingdom?" It was Zakarian who spoke that time.

"I'm not sure. We are sending some of our best to gather more information before we come to any conclusions."

"So, either way what do we do?" Alveen wondered. "If it is her and she's choosing to live with the enemy then trying to save her isn't really an option."

"We will have to discuss it further once we have all the evidence. Until then, I will believe my mother is missing or dead." With that Zakarian hastily stomped out of the throne room with Alveen on his tail.

"Zakarian, what is going on? Why are you being like this?"

"Because," he stopped dead in his tracks and faced her raising his voice, "They want us to believe that our mother is a traitor. I know you don't remember her, but I do, and I would never have thought of her to be a woman to switch loyalties. Betrayal is the ultimate crime to a family, and I would rather remember my mother as dead, than as someone who deceived and abandoned us." Alveen was left standing in the corridor watching her enraged brother disappear like a ghost, silently down the hall

She decided some fresh air would do her some good. Before she returned to her room she managed to fight through the maze of a palace to reach the outdoors. Walking down the moss covered ramp she decided to go back to where her accident happened. It wasn't a double moon and the protective barrier was up. She followed the stepping stones to a steep hill where a pathway was lit up and she could see the glimmer of the water at the end.

Her toes wiggled over the smooth pebble beach as she walked along the crashing waves, holding her gown and shoes between her fingers. In the distance she heard a long beautiful whistle. She stayed where she was and sat on the beach allowing the warmth of the sun to relax her.

"Banphrionsa?" Alveen opened her eyes at the native title and looked around. At first, she wasn't sure what to think or say to what was before her. In the water about knee deep was what appeared to be a pale blue head with a small fin along the back, gills along the neck and eyes that were a barren black. "Banphrionsa Alveen is back!" The creature squealed. Then that beautiful whistle rang out again and without delay a dozen more popped out of the water, all with what seemed to be a blissful reaction.

"I'm sorry, do I know you?"

"Oh, the accident. I forgot about that." The creature paused and slowly moved closer. "We are the mermaids of Palace Bay. No syragons here, I promise." The mermaid pushed herself up on her arms, which were lined with spined fins, and crawled out to where the waves crashed. Alveen was about five feet away from her now. "We used to be friends." Alveen now saw her whole body. Her torso was smooth like that of a fish's stomach. Gills lined her ribcage and right below where a normal person would have a belly button, Alveen admired the fist-sized metallic scales lining the muscular tail with a giant webbed semi-translucent fin.

"Oh my gosh. You're a mermaid."

"Yes." The mermaid looked at Alveen with a smile on her face, amused by her lack of knowledge.

"I'm sorry, I know I use to know you and of your kind but where I've been, mermaids are explained so different." Alveen watched as the others pulled themselves up onto the rocks nearby. They were almost alien like. "What was your name?"

"You can call me Shayah, our real names are not something your vocals can pronounce." She giggled and stared at Alveen. She noticed a small hole above Shayah's forehead and everything began to click.

"You use echolocation?"

"Mostly, yes."

"I don't mean to sound insulting by any means, but your physical appearances make much more sense to be a mermaid than what I have heard in stories."

"I have not heard any of these stories you talk of, but everything seems to have a purpose and works well for us." Shayah said bending her arms and flexing her fins. She was a hard creature to talk to and keep eye contact with, her eyes were darker than a starless night.

She rested on the pebbles, learning so much from the mermaids before deciding she should get back to her room. She had learned about how different the seas and bodies of water were there, about the syragon lair and where not to go. She even learned how to call for a mermaid if the time ever required it.

"I have enjoyed my time with you ladies so much and thank-you for teaching me all that you have. I really must return to my room for the night though. Enjoy the moonlight!"

Alveen waved as she headed towards the trail, smiling as the whistles softened when she put more distance between herself and the beach.

The steps were lined with a multitude of flowers, glowing in their own radiant shades resting on the grass below. She admired the bark on the cathedral like trees as they shimmered in the darkness. Even the moss had a slight glow to it as she gracefully climbed the slope entering the palace. She could feel the magic under her feet.

• • •

"Where have you been!?" Her brother's voice rang with concern and anger behind her as she approached the high, solid doors covered in recognizable engravings that opened to her bedroom.

"Out exploring, I had no more classes to attend and you left me alone in the hallways." She folded her arms with a matter-of-fact look glued to her face.

"I was worried about you. I didn't know where you went, and after getting news like that, what was I supposed to think happened?" he didn't give her time to respond. "I'm assigning a guard to you, you can still do as you please, but I would like someone with you all the time." Zakarian leaned against the wall letting his head fall backwards. "Tomorrow morning, I will have someone come pick you up and escort you to your courses and stay with you so you can do as you wish after."

"Zakarian, I am not a little girl. I understand your concern, but I do think rationally before I go anywhere. I do not need a full-time body guard."

"Sister, will you please do this for me. At least for a week. If it seems they are unnecessary after that, then we will talk about it." She was frustrated, her brother was treating her like a child that needed to be supervised, but she understood his concern.

The news didn't hit her as deep as him since she didn't remember her parents.

"Fine."

"Thank-you, sweet dreams sister." And he disappeared again. She rolled her eyes and walked into her room sliding off her new shoes, which she was so in love with she considered sleeping in them.

"Your Highness, do you need assistance getting out of your dress?" The young girl was waiting for her near her vanity.

"Yes please, if you don't mind." Alveen turned so her back faced the girl and felt the dress loosen up. "Thank-you" A bouquet of fully bloomed teal and white roses was placed next to her bioluminescent flowers from Samual. She walked over holding her gown close to her chest and read the note written on thick parchment paper tied to the vase.

'For the most beautiful Princess in our world and every other. Forgive me for not being able to tell you this in person. Yours, Samual.' It turns out he was thinking of her too. She smiled and walked to the closet closing the doors. She threw on another oversized shirt and leggings before joining the girl at the vanity. "I am so sorry. I've been so rude, what is your name?" Alveen asked the girl.

"Mysti, Your Highness." The girl answered, grateful that she was acknowledged.

"It is very nice to officially meet you Mysti and thank-you so much for helping me." Alveen watched the young girls face as she untwisted the braid in Alveen's hair.

"If you would like I can do sets of braids in your hair before you sleep, and in the morning your hair will have very beautiful curls?" Alveen thought for a moment, she was supposed to be getting a guard, maybe she would be lucky enough to have Samual assigned to her every day. She thought of his comment about how he loved her curls.

"Yes please, that is a wonderful idea." Minutes later Alveen had dozens of braids twisted into a bun on top of her head to make sleeping more comfortable.

"Do you need anything else, Your Highness?"

"No thank-you, go get some rest. I shall see you in the morning?" Mysti shook her head with a smile. Once she left the room Alveen couldn't help going to her balcony and looking down to see if her admirer was home. The lights were on and his cloak was hung up on the branch outside. Then walking around the porch was Samual, shirtless Samual to be exact. Alveen wasn't sure whether to look away or yell down to him. Before she could

● ● ●
103

make up her mind he was looking up at her and waving with that amazing smirk across his face. She could see him clearly enough to know he was wearing his reading glasses, making him look sexy and sophisticated again, and to know her assumptions about what was under his shirt were correct. The moonlight reflected off his smooth skin and she felt sinful just looking at him now. She waved back and walked into her room closing the doors behind her. Crawling into her bed, she tried to get that handsome man out of her head.

~CHAPTER VII~

JEALOUSY

"This looks amazing! Where did you learn this?" Alveen stared at Mysti in the vanity mirror admiring the curls that flowed along her skin and torso from the braids that Mysti had tied them in the night before.

"Well, my sister and I only have a few options for hairstyles. I would often wake up and redo our hair, and it would look fancy like this."

"It looks beautiful, thank-you." Mysti continued to work on Alveen's appearance. "What color dress should I wear today

Mysti? Would you help me pick something out?" Mysti's face lit up.

"Are you sure, Your Highness? I don't have a very good sense of beauty."

"Yes you do, here." She guided Mysti into the closet filled with exquisite gowns. "I wish you to be my friend Mysti, not just a servant." Mysti began to tear up.

"You are kind Your Highness." She looked at the dresses for a few moments. "May I suggest this gown, Your Highness?" Alveen reached for the gown Mysti pointed out. It was a chiffon sea foam green color with a high modest neckline, natural waist and a back that was covered in crossing straps. "It is very simple. One of your more casual dresses since you only have classes today."

"This is a very good choice Mysti, it will help me not stand out as much if I do go out into Cosaint."

"And it will bring out all of your natural beauty. Some of your dresses are so divine, everyone pays attention to the gowns and not to your face, Your Highness."

"I have noticed that." Alveen shook her head and slipped into the light weight gown. "What do you think of these shoes?"

She pulled out a gold pair of gladiator sandals that wrapped around her calves and up to her knees. The dress had a slit in it that went about mid-thigh on both sides, making her feel like some kind of warrior goddess.

"You look like a beautiful warrior, Princess."

"Thank-you for your assistance." A few knocks on the door and Zakarian pushed the door open slightly.

"May I enter?"

"Yes brother" Zakarian walked in with a large man behind him. He had to be about six feet tall as he stood near level with Zakarian. He looked much bigger as she noticed his oversized chest and arms. He was a very bulky man. Alveen wanted to giggle at how unrealistic he looked, but what was realistic here?

"And I thought you couldn't get more beautiful." Zakarian reached for her hand and kissed it. "I do like this look on you." He twirled her once and released her hand.

"Thank-you, I favor it as well." She put her hands on her hips and stood tall, "And who is this?"

"This is Jayuk, he is one of the strongest guards."

"It's an honor Banphrionsa. I hope you will enjoy your time while I am around." His voice was deeper than she was used to, but it didn't do that thing to her heart like Samual's did. *'Samual is probably much stronger though'* she thought to herself.

"I'm sure I will." She smiled and looked between the men. "Are we ready to go to my lesson?" Zakarian gestured after her. Jayuk walked out first and then walked along side of her. Alveen kept her composed act together. They walked in silence, Alveen keeping her pace a little faster than normal, pushing her shoulders back to give a confident and proud appearance.

"You can be very intimidating, Banphrionsa." He finally spoke when they were almost to the library.

"You think I'm intimidating?" She asked amused.

"You are confident and seem like an exceptional leader." He smiled at her and she could almost swear it was meant to be flirtatious. How would he know if she was a good leader?

"I appreciate that, Jayuk. I am not sure what Zakarian expected you to do while I'm in lessons but I'm sure you will find something. Now if you'll excuse me." She turned quickly making her dress twirl around her silky legs. Jayuk stared at her as she walked away. He decided to stick around and watch how she acted during her lessons. He stood back on the level above her watching as she got excited about something in every subject. When she was about done he walked down to the library doors to meet her.

"Wonderful lesson, Banphrionsa Alveen, you are making amazing progress and doing so well retaining all the information." Hilfyro said to her as they walked to the doors.

"Thank-you, I truly do find it all fascinating and if I am royalty I should probably know these things about -" She was interrupted before she could continue.

"Ready to go?" Jayuk asked.

"Yes. I suppose." She answered slightly irritated with him. "I look forward to our lessons tomorrow, Ollahm Hilfyro." They bowed to each other and she walked passed Jayuk, with him following right behind her and then stopped suddenly by one of the pillars. "I am not one to use my position to act superior, especially since I'm not quite sure what my position is, but please do not ever interrupt me again, especially while I'm talking to Ollahm." Alveen spoke bluntly to the man twice her size.

"I apologize; I didn't think I was being rude."

"You were. My studies are very important to me, and I expect you to respect that, especially since I'm stuck with you for the next week."

"Don't make it sound like such a bad thing." She rolled her eyes giving him an irritated glance to his response before she walked toward the entrance. "So where exactly are we going?"

"Aren't you just supposed to follow me and make sure I don't get hurt?" he nodded in understanding and followed her down to the bay first.

"How can you come back here after such a horrifying accident? Now I understand why Zakarian was concerned." He spoke as she began descending the natural staircase, his tone condescending.

"Because I don't remember it" she was in an irritable mood without much reason, "I find this area to be peaceful and reassuring, which is why I would guess, I use to come here a lot."

Jayuk looked out across the water as Alveen climbed a pile of boulders near the shore, taking a deep breath in and letting out a long melodic whistle. What was she doing? He hadn't meant to come off rude in the library, so he decided to approach her and try to discover her heart about the situation she was in.

"Banphrionsa?" He walked towards where she was positioned looking out over the bay.

"Yes?"

"Is something bothering you? I do apologize for coming off rude earlier, but I feel as if you are still unwelcoming to my presence."

"That would probably be because I am." She sighed, realizing her frustration was being misplaced. "It is not meant to be a personal offense to you; more that I am bothered that my brother thinks I need babysitting." She sighed, waiting for the mermaids to approach. "I know he's just trying to be a good big brother though." He stared at her with curiosity.

"You are fascinating, Your Highness."

"How so?"

"Well, you are beautiful, kind, very intelligent and not easily intimidated. And you seem to have a very relaxed personality compared to the other royals, if you don't mind me saying." Alveen was shocked to hear these things, not because she didn't believe them but because they came off as extremely flirtatious in his tone and she was most certainly not interested in this guard. She also couldn't tell him who she did have an interest in. As she was thinking of a response, she saw Samual training outside his home. Every part of her wanted to run to him, but she held herself back.

"I appreciate the compliments, Jayuk, and please forgive me if I'm reading this wrong, but if this is meant to be flattery, it will get you nowhere. I am otherwise engaged when it comes to relationships, so please take this as a friendly rejection."

"I understand, Your Highness, I apologize if I was out of line." Alveen looked back to where Samual was and he had disappeared from her view. Hopefully she would see him soon. "Um, Banphrionsa?" She turned and looked out into the water where Jayuk was looking. The mermaids were there.

"Banphrionsa! It's so wonderful to see you!"

"Likewise, Shayah. How is the bay today?" They spoke for a while. Jayuk seemed surprised at her interactions with them. He listened intently as the Banphrionsa spoke of how she used to love the sea on the world she had been on and wondered if this one was anything like the one she knew. Her beauty radiated when she was relaxed like she was here. He thought her rejection was just an independence thing, maybe she was not secure enough yet. After all, if the Banphrionsa was otherwise engaged or in any sort of relationship, surely the whole kingdom would know. He decided to take it slow, but make his interest known.

He watched as Alveen slid off the boulders and the mermaids disappeared under the surface. "You are most certainly intriguing."

"Intriguing. Fascinating. You just cannot help yourself, can you?" Alveen laughed shaking her head.

"Most royals wouldn't dare spend their free time with merfolk. They have always been considered suspicious and of low standings."

"That seems rather prejudice if you ask me. I was friends with them before also. I do not understand how status was ever saw as such a huge difference and a problem. Even back on Earth it was that way." She spun around quickly, unintentionally allowing her legs to be exposed. "And they are not low in my opinion. Though most of the elf cross breeds I have met are." She was stern with him and gave him a look, so he knew she was talking about him. He followed her down the path to the city, curious as to where her next adventure would take them.

"The training grounds? You honestly like watching these clumsy wannabes fall over each other with no skill?" She thought his arrogance couldn't possible get any more irritating, and apparently she was very wrong.

"Yes, I enjoy coming to the training grounds." She glared at him and folded her arms. "I enjoy watching the progression of future warriors that may someday be under my command, as I have just learned today in my courses." She couldn't tell him she was there to watch one specific warrior, she wasn't even sure when or if her and Samual would ever tell of their infatuation, if that was indeed what it was.

She spotted him a moment later. He was standing to the side observing the novices, though it seemed as if he was studying her and her body guard. Jayuk leaned down and whispered in her ear, "That's Samual, Head of the Palace Guard. It's said he talks a large game, but could never hold his own on the battle field." Samual's face grew stern as he watched what Alveen could only imagine looked like an intimate moment between her and Jayuk. Alveen was officially aggravated..

"Could you please escort me to my brother? I wish to have lessons with him." She glanced back at Samual, hoping she could speak with him soon. She did not wait for Jayuk as she nearly jogged back to the palace where she prayed she would find her brother to get her away from this obnoxious man. She could hear him trying to start conversation and he ran to her side, easily keeping up with her pace. Alveen ignored him, completely blocking out any of his comments. She was tired of hearing his voice.

Alveen raised her hand and pounded non-stop on Zakarian's personally etched high arched door.

"Alveen? What are you doing here?" Zakarian answered from the inside of his chambers.

"I would really like some time with you alone please. There is much we need to discuss." She smiled as if nothing was wrong but she just wanted a little freedom away from her assigned admirer. He shook his head and asked her to wait outside the room while he changed and excused Jayuk for the day. Jayuk gave Alveen a heartbreaking look, making her feel terrible inside.

"I hope I did not cross any lines today, Banphrionsa. I only wish for you to be safe and happy." Alveen's emotions swirled as he walked away. She had no interest in him, but she couldn't help feeling guilty and that maybe she crossed a line being overly rude to him.

"I hope I'm not interrupting." The voice forced goose bumps onto Alveen's skin knowing exactly who it was.

"Samual!" She spun around, not even knowing he was behind her, though she did not rush to hug him since her brother would be there at any moment. "I was hoping I could see you today."

"The training field wasn't enough?" He asked looking un-amused. She had never seen him so unhappy.

"Well, I wasn't sure if I would get to see you any other way, and it is not unusual for a royal to observe training."

"Did your new body guard enjoy it?"

"No, I don't think he did."

"What were you talking about?" He stood facing away, still stern. "When he whispered to you, what did he say?"

"He um.." she trailed off not wanting to repeat the insult to him. "He was just making comments. He wouldn't shut up all day, honestly."

"He cares for you."

"What? I think he may admire a future leader, but I doubt he has serious interest in me." This time, Samual couldn't keep his composure. He spoke to her as if he was disgusted.

"He hovers over you as if you are his prize. And it is only the first day he has been assigned to you." Her temper flared. How dare he address her like that, Princess or not. Even as an equal she wouldn't tolerate for someone to be so disrespectful. It was his job to hover over her.

"Is that concern or jealousy?" It was a comment she wanted to hold in, but she realized she was not that kind of girl, nor did she want to be the kind of leader that left things unsaid. He gave her a hurtful look.

"Either way it is obvious to see you find humor in it." He had opened up to her and though the hints may not have gotten through to her, he expressed his interest in her, and she acted as if he was nothing more than a citizen fawning over the long-lost Princess.

"Ah Samual! Is everything okay? What are you doing here?" Zakarian had emerged from his room dressed casually in jeans, dress shoes, a dress coat and plaid scarf.

"Everything is wonderful!" Samual managed to put a mask on over his hurt expression. "I was just coming to ensure the palace was secure when I ran into The Banphrionsa. We were just having a little discussion about schooling that was all."

"Oh, of course. Will I see you tomorrow?"

"Of course, I wouldn't miss it for the world." He walked away without a simple good bye to Alveen.

'What is going on tomorrow?" Alveen questioned. It was obvious Samual didn't want to talk further about it since he excused himself from the conversation, but Zakarian had no issues explaining.

"There is a hunting party. We will ride out and scout the area and see if we can find ourselves anything feast worthy." She was uninterested immediately. Not that she was against hunting, but she did not see them allowing a girl along, let alone in a dress. "You know, it may gain some respect if you came along. I know you are quite deadly with a bow and arrow."

"I shall think about it."

"So, what are we going to do today?"

"I was hoping you could start teaching me magic? At least the rules and guidelines so I am aware, and we can start sooner." He gave her a look admiring her persistence.

"I suppose we could. I would also like to take you to dinner in town tonight, if you have no plans?

"Ohh, that sounds most intriguing my dear brother." She smiled and grabbed his extended elbow, so he could escort her. It reminded her of their banter back on Inaitithe, something she missed dearly.

"We will start in the study, so I can teach you and there are no distractions." Alveen nodded following him through the halls in silence, enjoying not having Jayuk's annoying comments every few seconds. "Have a seat." He pulled out a chair that looked so comfortable she was afraid she might fall asleep while listening.

"So where do we start?" She asked anxiously folding her legs up in the oversized chair, careful to not expose too much of her skin with the slits her gown had.

"Like everything else, with the history." He smiled and turned around waving his hands until the correct books floated through the air and landed on Alveen's lap. "These are a few books that you can study, if you wish, in your free time. They will help explain better than I will." She began to flip through them as if they held the answer to a life altering question. "Our world was forged from magic. Our world was not the first, and no one knows how or when the first world was created. It was similar to the situation back on Inaitithe when we used the portals. Remember how we had to go to one of the areas which emulated the most magic, allowing us to perform such tasks? When our world was created it was through the overflow of magic from the first world. Due to the overflow, our world was slowly created, with that, each creature, until we learned to harness the magic. Especially when the original sorcerer and sorceresses started to use all of their power together, before the creation of the syragon. I'm talking way before that. No one knew the boundaries of magic, even the ones who pretended they ruled over it." Alveen listened intently though part of her still felt like she was listening to a fairytale. "All of the rules and guidelines for magic, are not put into place to prevent anything good from happening, they are put into place to prevent the inevitable. For example, you cannot create life, or simply take it away. Let's say, for example, something horrible happens and I die. You, being the powerful elven princess that you are, think you can bring me back, and in theory, you can."

"No way! Really?"

"Alveen, please listen. This is probably the most important of all of the lessons you will learn concerning magic." He continued when he knew she was focused. "In theory, you can bring me or anyone else back to life, but not without a consequence, and all magic has a price. We do not create anything or make anything vanish, we simply use our abilities to transfer energy and power from one thing to the next. So, if you bring me back to life, that life needs to come from somewhere else...

something that has the same energy and power as I do."

"What would that be?"

"Another royal elf. You see, everything in our world is alive and has energy and power, since it was all formed of magic, but you see, a tree would not have the same power or energy as that of a creature like us. It simply couldn't be transferred. If you were to try to use your ability to bring me back to life, it would not pull from the tree, but from you and before the magic would even have a chance to work through me, you would be dead too, making the whole endeavor pointless."

'So it is not able to be done?"

"Oh, it is, but it would end up being more like a sacrifice where someone willingly gave their life and you transferred the energy and power from them, to the dead. Now, it is only that complicated with living, breathing moving creatures. Plants, rocks, water, air, fire, all of that has both energy and power, but since they require so little of it, we can pull from our world, to help sustain it. I will show you an example on our way to dinner." He flipped through another book. "So, rule number one, summed up, is you cannot take or give life out of nothing. Rule number two, energy cannot be transferred through things too unalike, as I explained with the tree example. Rule three, which is more of a guideline, magic done through potions and spells take much more energy than those used from the elements, making elves much more powerful than sorcerers, sorceresses, warlocks or witches. And lastly, rule four, the magic we possess in this world is simple, it is not able to be used to manipulate the minds of others." He paused while Alveen took notes. "As much as we can do, most of it is rather limited to moving things, using any form of nature, air, fire or water, and anything you can create a potion or spell for, which brings us to a large loop hole in the rules. Elemental magic, such as we are capable of using, is things like the warriors would use. The only reason I am telling you these, so you understand the extent of self-defense that magic has. We can harness the air, essentially making someone suffocate, which is not technically taking someone's life in the magic handbook, they die of suffocation as they could without magic. We can harness wind and thrust it towards others, sending them flying backwards, possibly knocking them unconscious or simply moving them from where they are. We can harness fire, controlling it to one area, pushing it to another, controlling the heat of it and any other things. We can harness water, creating waves or paths, even control the rain. As far as the natural earth, you've seen that to work in the palace and the village. Both were created from elves manipulating trees, vines, plants and even the ground itself to form what they wish."

"That all sounds so amazing. Can you show me?" her excited tone reminded him of when she was young.

"Not today" he laughed. "But someday soon, I promise. One thing with all these though, is in elemental magic, it must be present. Air is easy to manipulate since it is always around, and wind you simply blow air or wave an arm and you have created even the smallest breeze to control, water is easiest by a body, but you can control a cup of water, bathtub or something like that as long as water is present, fire is the hardest, since you either need to start a fire or have one present. Some warriors have tricks if that's what they specialize in."

"So, no taking or giving life. Use elemental magic as often as possible since it takes less effort and energy from you, magic can't be used to manipulate people's thoughts, to use elemental magic an element must be present and transferring energy requires similar beings or objects. Is that the summary?"

"Yes, I guess that about covers it." He thought for a few seconds, "Oh! One other thing, Dorcha tribes cannot do magic for a number of reasons. Some of them have given the power inside them to the sorceress, giving her more strength but taking away their ability to yield it themselves. Since they are for the majority, similar beings, it is possible. She manipulates minds, though she does not need magic to do it, and they become willing to give their energy and power to her."

"This is all fascinating. So how does one possess magic?" She tried to push him to answer.

"Good try, but you're not ready yet." He switched some of her books out with the wave of an arm, teaching her more about the basics of energy and power, spells and even a few potion recipes. "Are you hungry yet?"

"Famished. Let's eat." She stacked her books up on her arms. "Ready?" he grabbed some of her books.

"How about we get someone to take these back to your chambers? I will call Mysti."

"You know her name?"

"Yes, I make it a point to know those around me by name."

"She really is so sweet, and might I mention, quite the beautician. She hand-picked this gown, did my hair and makeup."

"It has done a wonderful job on your appearance that is certain. That gown is amazing. You look like you are about to ride into battle, but in an elegant way."

"I suppose I should be flattered." She looked around as they walked out of the palace. "Where are we going?"

"Somewhere you use to love, let's see if that has changed." They approached a hill heading towards the bay. "I used to bring you here for picnics when we were younger." Alveen ascended to the top of the grassy hill. It overlooked the glimmering water reflecting a glorious sunset, looking as if someone had taken a pallet of all colors and tossed them into the clouds above. It was a change from the constant cover of the trees. "You used to love how the bay reflected the sky, you said it made you feel like you were flying." Her eyes reflected the sunset as she felt the full impact of what she could only assume was the magic this world truly had. Her heart pounded harder than she remembered, she felt the world under her feet vibrating with energy.

"This is so amazing. Where do we eat?" She turned, focused on how hungry she was, and saw he had a wicker basket hanging from his arm. "Aw." She smiled and sat down, anxious to see the contents.

"So what is your favorite part of all of this so far?" Zakarian asked his little sister.

"So many things. The people, the knowledge, how new everything is… and let's not forget the gowns." He laughed at her innocence. "What about you?"

"Well, I love that you are finally able to experience this life. But," he paused preparing to tell her the secret he'd been keeping. "I recently found out something both hurtful and exciting. It is a secret though and I'm hoping you will keep it between us?"

"Of course, I would never share your secrets." He took a deep breath.

"I have a daughter." He spoke quietly, looking in her eyes.

"What?" She exclaimed. She wasn't upset, but she had never even seen him with a woman. "Keep talking." she insisted.

"Before we were forced to leave, I was in love. I have been in love with this amazing woman. As the world would have it though, she is not pure blood elf, in fact she in not elf at all. Our parents approved, but our grandmother doesn't. Anyways, we had spent a few nights together before our departure, not knowing if we'd ever see each other again, and one romantic evening led to a beautiful little girl that I haven't gotten the chance to love like a father should."

"I never knew.. that's so sad. What her name?"

"The girl or my daughter?"

"Both!"

"Malika is the girl, beautiful black hair. She is fairy and mermaid. Our daughter is Tanilly. Long, blonde hair and the most precious pink eyes, like newly discovered gems."

"So, now that you have a daughter do you plan on telling grandmother?"

"Well, I do have to, especially if I want Tanilly to have any chance at the throne or higher respect. Though she will automatically get it being half elf, not that anyone would know that if I don't do what I need to." He sighed then looked into Alveen's eyes. "Are you mad?"

"No, I mean I could be disappointed that I didn't know but it's not like you had much of a chance." She laughed. "Can I meet them sometime?"

"Of course, we haven't told Tanilly that I'm her father yet. We want to see what's going to happen once I tell grandmother. But then yes of course, though I'm pretty sure she knows you as The Princess and would be thrilled to see you."

Alveen sat quiet. Her brother just admitted a huge secret to her, that was way worse than her flirtation with Samual. No one knew but she wanted to tell someone. Maybe she should talk to Samual first, if he would even be willing to talk to her. She decided it was best to keep quiet for now, until she knew where his feelings were.

"That I understand."

"I would like to run something else by you." She looked at him anticipating whatever was coming next, "I would like to ask Malika to marry me. I know you need to meet her first to get a full picture, but I never in my wildest dreams expected her to have waited for me all these years, though it really isn't that long in this world I suppose."

"I don't need to meet her to know you've made a good choice. If she's worth waiting for all this time, she must mean a lot to you."

"Thank-you." He paused and looked out over the bay before he brought up his next point. "Oh! Speaking of which, I haven't spoken with grandmother yet, and please don't cut my head off for suggesting this, but it is tradition, you are of age to be accepting suitors."

"Suitors?"

"Yes. Men who wish to court you in order to gain your hand in marriage. I know you feel you are too young, and I agree, but it never hurts to court for a while and see if you find your match." All she wanted to tell him was that she may have already that, and she didn't want anyone, especially anyone like Jayuk, having the ability to court her. There had to be a way around it.

"Um... actually..." She paused trying to quickly figure out how to avoid it.

"Is there something wrong?"

"Yes." She let out before she could politely think of a response. "You see, there is a gentleman that I believe I have quite strong feelings for."

"Oh? And who would this be and why have you not said anything to me?"

"Let's just say I am not certain on his feelings towards me, and before I bring any names into the equation, I would like to know if it's even worth mentioning. But until I am sure of the direction of this possible relationship, I would like for this whole suitor issue to not be mentioned... maybe it can all be avoided." He paused studying her, hoping she would give a small detail as to who this gentleman was. She was busy studying and always alone. Or was she? Did she go to see someone when she was in

Cosaint every evening? How did they meet? Questions whirled inside his head as he began to think who it could be. Hopefully not her professor. Jayuk seemed to show interest in her, maybe it was her new guard? Did he unknowingly play match maker?

"I can understand out of courtesy for the two of you, that you would want to get things worked out and make sure you are on the same page before we make things messy and complicated." He looked at her. "Who is it?"

"I am not telling you until I know the status." She jokingly gasped at his persistence.

"Is it that new guard? Jayuk? He seemed interested.." Her face snarled.

"Ugh" she groaned, "No way. He was flirting and trying to flatter me all day. He infuriates me, he's judgmental and rude. I asked to come see you as a way of escaping him, though this was much needed time together."

"So, I am way off. Good to know."

"Please don't look into it. He is an amazing man. Up until today I was positive I knew where we stood, but we did have quite the disagreement today, due to Jayuk being over flirtatious, so I am hoping to eventually get it worked out."

"Understood. I will drop it until you are ready to tell me. Please let this suitor know that it is proper etiquette to ask permission to court first."

"I will relay the message if necessary." She smiled and leaned on his shoulder looking up at the star filled sky. It looked so different. You could see what looked like planets and galaxies from where they were. There was so much detail when you gazed upon it; you couldn't help but become curious. "Should we head back?"

"Yes, of course. You do have courses tomorrow." He leaned down to the ground. "Wait a second, I forgot to show you one of my favorite things about magic." He leaned down and pulled a dead flower out of his pocket. "The world is always growing, and this is a form of magic that helps the elements, making it one of those rare occasions…" he paused, laid the flower down on the ground and made a large circle with his palm down over it, then stood back up. Streams of fog floated from the ground as though gravity had shut off. Within seconds the once dead flower, turned into a small rose bush. The roses were a blush color, and they sparkled as the fog drifted back into the ground. "That we can give life." He reached over and picked a large fully bloomed rose and handed it to her.

"I can't wait to do that." She exclaimed as she inhaled the aroma of the new born rose. He smiled at her and escorted her back to her chambers. "It was a lovely evening. Thank you for everything."

"Anytime. We will need to make a habit of this. Please keep me informed on your suitor."

"I will." She pushed herself up onto her tip toes and kissed his cheek. "I love you, I will see you soon."

"Yes, you will." He bowed and walked away as she opened her door. She gazed around her room, still unable to get over how detailed and profound it was. Noticing her bouquets were still on her vanity, she walked to them and added her rose to the teal flowers.

"Adding another man's flowers to mine… way to hit a man when he's down." Alveen spun quickly. "From a suitor? Is that what I heard?" Samual was standing on the balcony, leaning against the door frame, looking directly at her with a blank face. He looked composed, like there was nothing bothering him, but she saw the fires of jealousy burning in his eyes at the thought of another man trying to win her heart.

"You're here. I thought I would have to hunt you down." She wanted to smile as she stared at his beautiful features, but she was far too upset with his actions to give him the satisfaction of making another rude comment to her. She knew it wasn't entirely her fault. She had rejected Jayuk, defending Samual and not once did she ever show interest in him, but somehow Samual saw otherwise.

"Apparently it's I that has to do the hunting since so many others are prowling after you."

"Okay, this is ridiculous." She was through with this immaturity "I shouldn't have to explain myself to you, but I will out of respect." How dare he make it sound like she was so flirtatious with so many men. She slowly walked towards him as she defended herself, raising her voice. "First, Jayuk flirted with me and was heavily rejected, multiple times. In fact, I even informed him I was otherwise engaged, though he didn't seem to get the hint. When you saw him whispering to me, he was insulting you. The one man I care about in that sense, I defended you and walked away. I didn't want to tell you earlier because I don't like to repeat rumors. He is obviously insecure. Second, the flower was from Zakarian, which is where I've been all evening, because I'm sure your curious, and it was him who walked me back, and *you* are the suitor he was referring too." She was flustered and frustrated, her breath was heavy, and she didn't know how to continue, though she was pretty sure that's not how it should have started. He stood there as if he was in shock. She ran her hands over her face, walked to her bed, sitting down, waiting for him to say something.

"I...I'm sorry." He spoke soft. She had never heard him this way before. "I was childish, and yes, a bit jealous. I was jealous that he got to stand next to you in public and spend all day with you, and it seemed as if you were flaunting that when you showed up at the training field." He stood straight in the doorway of the balcony and walked over to where Alveen sat. She was now staring up at him as he apologized, with a hurt expression in her eyes. She couldn't stay mad at him, his dark eyes made her melt the moment he looked at her. "Will you accept this apology with a dance?" he extended a hand for her. Without hesitation she pulled herself close to him, holding his strong hand while her other arm rested over his toned shoulder. He twirled them out onto the balcony that was draped in moonlight. Her dress, once again, unintentionally exposed both of her legs as they twirled. The crisp night air floated along her skin with every movement. Samual leaned down to her neck and began serenading her the sweetest love song she had ever heard. With every word, his breath against her skin made her shiver with delight. His hand rested at the small of her back, just below where her back was exposed. He moved his hand up a few inches, so his warm palm rested on her now icy skin from the cool breeze. He began to run his fingers from her shoulder blades to the small of her back, like he was innocently treasuring the feel of her exposed skin.

When he finished his song, he leaned against the thick concrete railing of the balcony still holding her. "That was beautiful. I didn't know you could sing."

"Only for you, don't reveal my secret." he still spoke softly, but this time there was flirtation behind it as the mood lightened. She leaned against his chest and he tilted his head down, their foreheads nearly touching as they were only inches apart. "So, you are otherwise engaged? And who would this lucky man be?"

"Well, he's rather dashing. Probably the most handsome man I have ever laid eyes on. Speaking of eyes, his are so filled with passion." She looked up into his gleaming irises again as she described them. "He is extremely tough, and sensitive at the same time. He's quite amazing at picking out flowers and showering a girl with affection, he treats me like a princess" she winked and went on, "Oh and he's Head of the Palace Guard." He smiled.

"He sounds monotonous and dreary."

"He is neither of those, I promise that."

"So, does he know you are supposedly engaged with him?"

"Well that's the thing, you see. My brother tells me I'm of age to accept suitors to court me-." She leaned back and looked at him, "But I informed him that I already have a suitor, but I would not tell him the name of this man until I was certain that him and I were on the same page as far as what our relationship is." She stepped back enjoying the breeze and spun around. "Oh, and this said suitor is to be informed that if he wishes to properly court me, he must first have proper etiquette and ask my brother." He watched her intently, like if he missed a move she made, he would be missing a wonder of the world or a rare phenomenon. He watched her silky legs peek out of her goddess like gown as she walked back towards him. Her leg was exposed as she leaned into his chest and her hair smelled like the salty bay. He wrapped one arm around her waist, pulling her into his chest, and ran the other hand down her side to her exposed leg. He gently trailed his fingers along her skin and she turned her head watching his hand adore her. Alveen looked up at him.

"So where do we stand Samual Reignsbach?"

"I actually wanted to talk about this, but I wasn't sure when to bring it up." He sighed, "I would very much so like to publicly court you. I do not see anything going wrong in our courting, and I would like you to know that I do intend to marry you one day, when we are ready. I promise I will be a complete gentleman, your brother can even chaperone our escapades, if he wishes to be traditional, it does not matter to me. I did not want to speak with him until I had a chance to make sure you were okay with me pursuing this course." Her head was resting on his shoulder with her forehead touching his neck.

"I would wish for nothing else." He let a big breath out, like he had been holding it in the whole time he spoke. He pulled her in for a warm embrace. "Mrs. Alveen Reignsbach, I think I could get use to that."

"I should let you get some sleep. I will speak with Zakarian tomorrow." He kissed her forehead as he stood back up, following her to the threshold. "By the way," he put his lips only inches from her ear, "You look absolutely stunning in that gown." She turned her head, placing a kiss on his cheek. He gasped sarcastically. "Already? Mrs. Reignsbach you're moving so quickly. I cannot handle this." Alveen giggled as she watched his cloak float behind him as he departed her chamber.

She closed her door and took a deep breath. It took her a minute to get out of her gown and shoes and into her night outfit. At her vanity she attempted to wipe off the small amount of makeup she had on before she got under her covers. She had much to learn still about her new suitor but so far, he was that only man she had ever felt this way about. She tried to empty her mind and drifted off to sleep knowing she had a long day ahead of her tomorrow.

~Chapter VIII~

Courting

Samual woke and stretched as he always did. Since he did so much training, it was essential for him to warm up before he went to the grounds and began his day. He was out on the wrap-around balcony doing push-ups, sit ups, jumping jacks, burpees and stretches one last time before leaving. He had a busy day planned. Shortly he would be joining some men from the village on a hunt, including Zakarian, who he also had to inform that he was interested in courting his younger sister. He knew he would have time when he returned to take over a large group of novices as well.

It was not like Samual to over think situations, but all he could think about while getting ready that day was if Zakarian rejected his request. What would he and Alveen do if they were rejected the chance to grow closer? Would they still secretly meet or would she end it immediately? Maybe he could convince her to run away with him. He had to stop thinking about it before he drove himself to insanity. He had other things to focus on at the moment.

He descended the ladder to his home and followed the trail into the village and towards the palace. Zakarian was standing at the top of the ramp waiting for the men.

"Samual! So glad you could make it!" Zakarian exclaimed at he approached. He was greeted with a brotherly hug.

"I'm glad I could get out of my early morning duties" he joked, "I plan on going into Cosaint for dinner this evening after training, would you care to join me and catch up? It has been too long. Since your return we have both been busy." Samual knew he had to talk with him privately; this hunt was not the time to bring up such a delicate matter.

"That's a splendid idea. I have much I need to inform you of! There is much that has gone on." Only moments later Samual was taken by surprise. "Ah there she is!" Alveen walked out onto the ramp looking like The Princess he remembered her to be. Her hair was tied in small braids on the crown of her head to keep it out of her face, but the rest of her loose curls hung over her one shoulder. She wore tall flat boots, fitted dark emerald pants that had to have been made for her here being as they were a rare material meant to be flexible and durable. At her hips rested a brown leather belt sitting behind a quiver. The tight black long sleeve shirt she wore enhanced the toned muscles in her arms and was underneath a dark brown hooded vest that was zipped to right below her bust. Since she had returned she had only been in gowns and jewelry, this was the Alveen he missed so much.

"No gown today, Banphrionsa?" Samual asked casually.

"I assume it would get in the way. Especially if I intend to out shoot the Head of the Palace Guard." She sent him a wink as Zakarian looked over to the approaching men. "Zakarian invited me, I didn't decide I was going until this morning though. I must admit, I am loving being out of those gowns."

"You look much more comfortable." Samual spoke walking over to join the group. He leaned down as he passed her, "And good luck outshooting me." He winked back and motioned for her to join them. They had all rode up on their alicorns which they would ride or fly into the hunting territory. They were truly beautiful creatures. He watched as Alveen turned and admired some of them up close. He walked away to go get the alicorn that had missed Alveen so much.

"Thank you all for showing up on time. In case you have not noticed, the Banphrionsa will be joining us today. She is new to our customs; please give her the benefit of the doubt as she is still learning. I do know she is a good shot, so let's not leave her out of the fun gentlemen." The men bowed looking for her as she walked to join Zakarian at the front of the group. "Let's be on our way." Zakarian turned to Alveen. "You my dear, finally get to meet Allicent." She turned around and Samual was approaching with a solid black shimmering alicorn. Samual had taken care of Allicent since Alveen left. He looked solid black but when he lifted his wings, underneath was pure white and everything about the creature had a teal shimmer, just like Alveen's eyes. His horn was silver with that same sparkle as the sun reflected off it.

"This is Allicent. He has been waiting for you for a very long time." Samual introduced him. "I've been caring for him while you were gone. You used to love flying him." He watched Alveen step up to the magnificent creature and fall in love all over again. Samual turned around and started gearing up the alicorn for a flight. "Now, obviously it's been a while for you, but he remembers exactly what to do. Alveen." Samual looked into her eyes trying to get her attention. "Trust him. He knows what he's doing, and he will not hurt you." She smiled and shook her head, then looked back up into Allicent's eyes. The Alicorn was hesitant but began to get excited and playfully stomped his front hooves and rub against Alveen when he recognized her.

"He's so beautiful."

"Alright, let's go. Everyone is waiting." Alveen walked towards Samual and climbed onto the Allicent's back, placing herself in front of his enormous wings. "Zakarian and I will be flying near you." She was hardly paying attention to him.

Quickly Samual hopped on his alicorn, Beastil, and pulled back on the reigns. He flew past Alveen and up into the sky. He circled above for a few moments while Zakarian taught her the basics. Gradually the group launched into the sky and circled until they were all there. Alveen didn't take long to catch on, but Samual kept his eye on her in case anything went wrong.

The wind rushed by them and they soared through the sky, above the world. Though Samual had made this journey many times, Alveen had never been airborne in this world and her face reflected pure awe. Below you could clearly make out the bay that the palace sat near and the glimmering waterfalls sporadically placed through the mountain range. The canopy of the tress held creatures as they played in the warm sun. She looked to Samual and realized he was smiling ear to ear as he watched her. They began their decent. Samual made sure to lean back so Alveen could see what he was doing. Allicent could probably land by himself, but he knew Alveen would attempt to help.

Samual gracefully landed and turned to watch as she flew in behind him. Everyone else had already landed and started to spread out. Only moments passed before Allicent's hooves touched the forest floor. She looked like a natural, like she never forgot.

"That was so amazing! Why have neither of you taken me flying yet?" She questioned, still excited. He rolled his eyes at the question. It had only been a couple weeks in time that she was accustom to and everyone had been busy most of the days.

"Alright, so this is pretty simple. We're all going to spread out with a decent amount of space between us. We ride the whole time. If you see anything worth shooting, shoot it. We have most animals you would be use to such as moose, elk, deer and smaller animals. We will be close by still, or one of us can ride near you if you would prefer. If you hit something, whistle loudly. We will collect your kill, load it onto Allicent and move on as quick as we can." She shook her head. She was a natural at archery and she had been on hunting drives before with a high school friend who invited her to her families hunting camp one year.

She seemed so relaxed. Seeing her defend herself last night, being outspoken again, was like she was The Princess he remembered, just grown up, and now she had feelings for him.

Samual scanned the area, looking for anything large enough to feed a few families. The tree roots were uplifted out of the ground, the ground for the most part was flat and the towering trees waved in the steady breeze. He heard rustling in the leaves ahead. His eyes saw the antlers of a glorious elk. As he drew his bow back, he could see Alveen pushing herself up so she was standing on Allicent's back, and she swiftly drew back hers. She remembered her breathing, took her time to aim and slowly released. The elk dropped dead in its tracks before Samual even had a chance to aim. She slowly brought her bow down to her side and gave him a challenging smile. She jumped down off the alicorn's back and let out a long whistle. Samual and two other elves rushed to her side, congratulated her on the massive beast she had brilliantly shot, and helped her load it down on to Allicent's back.

"This can't possibly be safe for him to ride with that much weight." Alveen commented with concern.

"Trust me, this boy has carried much more than this. Alicorn's are known for their superior strength, just as elves are. That's one of the many reasons we have teamed up with them." Samual answered as he brushed off his shirt. He could see she was unsure. "How about you and I go back and unload this at the butcher? Then Allicent doesn't have to carry it as long." She smiled approving of his plan. He approached Zakarian and got his approval to leave the group with Alveen. "Alright. Hop on." Alveen swung her leg over and immediately turned around heading towards where they landed. They maneuvered through the mountain range until they reach the familiar body of water below them. Samual had to get in front of her so she would know where to land in Cosaint.

Samual pointed to a grassy field as they began their decent, motioning for Alveen to follow. "Your Highness! It is an honor to meet you." The butcher yelled as they landed behind his shop. He was of average height, shiny black hair, and pale pink eyes.

"Banphrionsa Alveen, this is the village butcher Masgo. Fairy and elven. Masgo, Banphrionsa Alveen went on the hunt with us today and wishes to turn her kill over to you." She swung her leg over and landed elegantly on the grass below.

"It's so nice to meet you. I apologize, I am trying to make my way around the village to meet shop owners." She bowed.

"Is this your kill, Banphrionsa?" The butcher looked surprised.

"Yes. Is there something wrong?"

"It is not often that women join the hunts, and it is rare that they come out with anything, especially such a beautiful beast. I will use every ounce of this creature."

"Do you think you could make a blanket from the hide, Masgo? For the Banphrionsa?" Samual requested.

"That would be wonderful if that's something you are able to do. And I wouldn't mind having the antlers." She said almost embarrassed.

"I can most certainly do that for you Banphrionsa. The meat, bones and organs are to be donated?" He questioned looking between Samual and Alveen.

"Yes, she would very much appreciate that." Samual answered for her.

"It will be done!" He bowed and called Allicent over so he could hoist the elk and begin his cuts. "It was wonderful to meet you, I hope to see you again soon Banphrionsa!" Masgo said as he walked into his shop to gather tools.

Samual gathers the reigns for Allicent and Beastil so he could return them to the stables. "What happens with the donated meat?" Alveen asked him.

"It goes to family's who may not have enough to eat, or need the extra protein. Many families around here farm or hunt themselves. Many even live off of simply what they plant. For some people that is not enough, and the palace raises enough livestock to generally feed everyone in it, and donate some. So the kills of any royal is generally donated to the village."

"That seems like a very good plan that's in place. I like it." She paused and started petting Beastil. "So when do you plan on approaching Zakarian?"

"Him and I are meeting for dinner, after my training. I plan to talk to him then." He stopped in front of the stables and looked down at her. "Is that okay?"

"Yes, of course. I was just curious."

"I will come to you as soon as we are finished. I promise." He smiled and kissed her forehead. "I will put these two gentlemen away, you need to get to your courses. I will see you tonight."

"I'm looking forward to it." She walked off in the direction of the palace. This day could not have started off better for Samual. After tying up the alicorn's he made his way to the main path of the village leading to the training grounds.

"Samual! Samual! Are you going to train today?" A young boy ran out from his home and walked alongside him. His name was Triton and he greeted Samual every morning. He was young still, but over the course of their many conversations he learned that he wished to be a warrior someday.

"Yes, I am. Are you going to watch me train today?"

"Yes! I do wish I could join you."

"One of these days, young Triton, I will give you a personal one on one lesson. Does that sound fair?"

"Yes sir! When will I know?"

"I will come find you. We will spend all day training and I will teach you to fight and defend your family." Triton's face lit up with joy thinking of wielding a weapon or being able to do magic. He walked alongside the young boy until he reached the training grounds. "This is where we part young man. Will I see you tomorrow morning?"

"As always, but my mother wishes to cook you lunch today, will you join us?"

"I think that can be arranged." He smiled and ran his hand through the boy's shaggy hair as he walked away to meet his new pupils.

"Welcome novices. I hope you are all prepared for what is to come. We will take on weaponry today. You will be learning how to strike and to defend yourselves, and this afternoon, we will test you." The young warriors cheered and stretched while waiting instructions. "First, I will have my young apprentice here be my assistant. Triton, will you join us?" The young boy hurriedly got to his feet and he ran over to Samual.

"Yes sir? What can I do?"

"You will be my partner today. I will show you basic defense moves, but you must promise only to use them if your life is in danger. Promise?"

"Yes sir." He stood still with his hands at his side.

"Alright then." Samual had Triton try to defend himself from faux attacks, then properly showed him, and the novices, how to execute each defense technique to ensure, no matter the opponent's size or skill, they will be able to protect themselves.

The training went on for a good portion of the day until Triton's mother came to get him for lunch. "Let's all take a break, eat a meal and we will meet back here to do a real test on what you've learned." Samual walked over with Triton. "It's nice to see you again, Layla."

"You as well Samual, what are you teaching my son now?"

"Defense. No worries, nothing violent." He winked at Triton who giggled. Layla was an older woman, who had taken Triton in after his biological mother had died during the birth of his younger brother, who also did not make it through the birthing. She admired Samual for taking Triton under his wing and giving him the attention and role model that was much needed.

"Are you joining us for lunch?"

"Yes ma'am, if you are alright with that. I can make do if you did not prepare for me."

"Oh Samual, there's always enough for you." She smiled and took Triton's hand leading him back to their home. Layla was an amazing cook, she could make any meal and it tasted better every time. He passed the time eating his meal by joking with Triton, learning about why he wanted to learn to fight. He was a spirited young boy and Samual loved him like a little brother.

"You know you can't come with me for the afternoon training, right?"

"Oh! Oh! Are you going through the portal!?" Samual laughed at his excitement.

"Yes, we are." He leaned down closer to him, 'Will you be waiting when I get back?"

"Oh no, not today lad. You have chores." Layla answered for him.

"Oh… no I will not be." His face dropped and he frowned with disappointment.

"That's alright; every man needs to learn how to help in the house. There is no shame in doing chores and helping your mother, do you understand that?"

"Yes sir." He smiled and ran off to play.

"Thank-you for lunch Layla. I must return to my novices, I suppose they will be waiting for me to finish the day."

"Thank-you Samual" He looked back at her puzzled, "for the love and attention you give that little boy." He bowed to her.

"It's my pleasure."

"You would be an amazing father, Samual. When will you be finding yourself a beautiful lass?" he blushed at the question.

"Hopefully much sooner than you think." She got excited at his comment. "But you must promise that you will make the meal at my wedding." She shook her head.

"Get back to work." She smiled as he ducked out of the house. Her modesty made him smile but he walked out the open doorway towards the group of novices waiting for him.

"Alright, the moment most novices wait for their entire training career. Does everyone know how to travel through a portal?" Everyone shook their head informing him that they did. "Perfect. When you get to the other side, wait for me and my instructions, you will not start without my command or you will be immediately removed from my training program, are we clear?"

"Yes sir" they yelled in unison. He motioned for everyone to get together. They all placed their hands on their neighbors back and began chanting in the native language. Slowly the breeze started to pick up, swirling around the large group like a tornado. The air above them turned into a spiraling pool as they each began to dive through, until Samual was the last one. He kept his eyes open and he was pulled through. Landing perfectly on his feet, his boots hit a field of tall grass. Many of the novices were on their butts or standing up waiting for him.

"Well done. Now does anyone know why we travel here for training?" no one answered. "Here is a little history lesson that you may enjoy. This is thought to be the first world ever created. It is free of life forms like us, the only life you find here, is the elements. This world radiates energy." He held his hand out, twisted his wrist and lifted his palm towards the sky. With the simple motion the ground rumbled, and monstrous roots twisted and bloomed into trees as they emerged from the ground. A warm breeze brushed across every novice's face, with his other hand he pushed downward and rain fell to the ground. He snapped his fingers and fire appeared in his palm. Then with a single clap, everything froze in place. The raindrops paused in mid-air, the fire was extinguished, the breeze disappeared and the trees towered above. "This world doesn't necessarily follow all of the rules of our world. This world *is* magic. You are here because I expect you all to fight your hardest, to fight like you would an enemy, if you are to be in the Palace Guard, you must be ready to kill." He paused making sure to get the full effect of their duties. "This world allows us to do that, with no real consequences. If you are hurt, you heal, if you are stabbed in the heart, you will be healed, if you are decapitated, you are healed. This world provides so much energy, it is impossible to die."

"Why don't we live here or bring our dying here?" one of the men asked.

"Simple. This world has been sustained without us or any other creature around to mess up its natural balance, if we live here, we screw it up. And taking a dying soul through a portal will kill them before they get here, it would be pointless. This world will not bring back the dead, but it will heal before they are dead, if the injury occurs here. For example." He grabbed his dagger and without blinking, sliced his arm. Gasps escaped from a few of the young warriors, but soon were replaced with awe as the drops of blood vanished from his wounds within seconds. It was as if nothing had happened. "Now, I will say, the worse the injury, the longer it takes to heal. So please don't decapitate anyone or cut off limbs if you can help it. They will take hours to heal. If it's bad enough it may even take a full day." He stepped back and observed. "You may begin" The young warriors lunged at each other, though none of them fell to the ground, the magic in the world healed the slices and stabs their opponents landed. Samual observed as the blood evaporated into the sky.

~Chapter IX~

The Inevitable

When Alveen left the hunting party she headed straight for the library to start her courses. She was excited with her skills, and that she proved she was worthy of hunting with the men in the village. She also knew she was to learn more about customs today with Ollahm Hilfyro.

"Ah! Banphrionsa! You're early!" He said excitedly standing to greet her. He bowed deeply out of respect keeping eye contact. "Lesson one. This is how any man should greet you. The deeper the bow the more respect and eye contact is crucial as it shows you have their attention and that they value you. I don't teach that royals are more important, though you are a rare species and are at the top of our hierarchy. Everyone from the bottom to the top has an important position and all are important." She stood there listening. "Be we will start in a moment. How was the hunt, Banphrionsa?" She began to get excited thinking about it again.

"Oh! It was amazing. I flew Allicient for the first time since my return, which was magical. And I had the first kill of the hunt. Magso is working on turning the hide into a blanket and getting me the antlers for my chamber. Everything else was donated."

"Ah that is wonderful. You are helping feed those with your generosity. Congratulations on your success today." He smiled, "Are we ready to begin?"

"Yes please. I am eager to learn my place and the customs here." She walked around the table and sat in the tall velvet lined throne adjacent to him, crossing her legs. "So, eye contact is good?"

"Most certainly. Now for a lady such as yourself, a deep curtsy in your in a gown, or a bow if you are dressed as you are now, the eye contact shows they respect your ascend to the throne. An extra show of loyalty is this," he reached his arm out, twisted his wrist and brought his arm down as he was bowing. "not many do this anymore, but it was used long ago"

"How should I be greeting my grandmother formally?"

"Ah, Queens or Kings would be slightly different. Since they have made it through the trials to become a King or Queen, you will dip down on one knee as you bow, and raise your forearm horizontally to them, then stand. Sometimes circumstances make it difficult to do so, such as a fitted gown, and then you would bow but make a wide circle with your right foot, to show an effort as more than a simple bow. But that is mainly for females at formal events."

"Okay so, in a normal situation I would do.." She trailed off acting it out. "that?"

"Yes, perfect form. It is very easy. Now in a fitted gown?" Alveen made a wide bow with her arms but brought her right foot to the side and meeting it back in the middle as she rose. "You're a natural."

He continued to go over different terms, greetings for different species, like a centaur does not wave, but places a fist over their heart. She was grateful to be learning all of this.

She managed to be undistracted the rest of the afternoon but as soon as she walked out of the library she had now come to know as a sanctuary she could go to think, she had nothing else to keep her mind distracted. She mindlessly wandered the palace with Jayuk silently in tow. It was going to be fine, Zakarian had no reason to tell Samual no.

She quickened her pace in the direction of the training grounds. Seeing Samual would at least give her some peace of mind.

"Where are we going?" Jayuk asked, nearly jogging behind her.

"I have an interest to watch the training today." Jayuk was confused as to why she insisted on visiting the grounds so often, but he followed her without questioning her motives.

When they arrived at the training grounds no one was around. A woman stepped out of a home nearby wearing a pale blue long sleeve shirt and dark grey fitted pants. The woman began walking towards her. "Banphrionsa! What brings you to this end of the village today?"

"Oh, hello. Um." She paused not really wanting to act suspicious, but nodded her head as she had just learned was the proper way for her to greet her citizens. "Have you seen Samual, Head of the Palace Guard? I was wishing to speak with him."

"Oh yes! My son is fond of him. He is training through the portal for the rest of the afternoon. I would assume they would be back in the next few hours though."

"Oh wonderful. If you see him when he returns will you tell him I stopped by, please?" Alveen asked with a sweet smile.

"Of course, Your Highness." The woman said with a deep bow in her casual outfit. With that, she leisurely walked back across the village, enjoying the smell of freshly made foods from some of the nearby bakeries and restaurants. One of them had a scent that made her mouth water simply passing by. She could not resist walking in. She had not gotten to know many of the villagers, but she hoped she would be the kind of leader that was one with her people.

"Banphrionsa, what an honor!" The tall gentleman behind the wood carved counter yelled in excitement. "Your Highness, you are much more beautiful than they describe. I heard you did well on the hunt this morning, congratulations!" He bowed to her and continued, "What can I do for you today?"

"I'm actually here because it smells so amazing walking by. What is it that teases my senses?" She walked closer, leaning on the smooth wood grain countertop that that separated them.

"Ahh." An enormous smile filled his face as he stood upright and walked towards the ovens. "And I thought you were here on business."

"Not at all. I am simply trying to learn the village." She smiled still standing at the counter. The lean man pulled a pan of small white cakes out of the oven.

"These, Banphrionsa, are something my great grandmother use to make. I do not sell them, but I would be honored if you would try one."

"Yes please! What are they exactly?" She leaned over trying to watch him put together his own form of a masterpiece. He flipped the small moist cake onto a plate and drizzled red and purple syrups over it, topping it off with a small dollop of some sort of cream and assorted berries. The steam began to melt the cream within mere moments. He walked back over with the plate and fork. "This looks amazing."

"It is a simple cake; secret family recipe." What she tasted did not line up with his words. There was nothing simple about this cake. When she cut it open there was a thick layer of what looked to be jam that had been cooked inside of it, and everything melted so perfectly together.

"What is your name?"

"Fenryr, Fenryr Vilkan, Your Highness."

"Fenryr, this is the most amazing dessert I have ever tasted in my lifetime. If I were to come back, do you think you could make this for me again? And would you mind giving me something to wrap this up with?"

"Absolutely Banphrionsa! I would be honored to have a special-order item, just for you!"

"Then please, expect me to be back for another within the week. I would appreciate if you could make them fresh? I will be willing to wait."

"Of course. I would do no less than my best for you."

"Thank-you sir, I look forward to trying more of your delicious creations." She bowed, realizing she was still in her attire from hunting this morning, and walked out of the store holding the remainder of her wrapped cake, hoping to share it with Samuel. Maybe Fenryr could make the wedding cake.

Jayuk followed her around the palace as she looked for Zakarian, and she still had not heard from Samuel, leaving her only other option to go back to her chambers and wait. She planned on studying the books Zakarian had given her and impressing him at their next session.

As Jayuk and Alveen approached her chambers, they noticed the door slightly ajar. "It was probably Mysti, no need to worry." Alveen assured Jayuk.

"You Highness, it is my duty to keep you safe. Please allow me to check inside before you rest for the evening." It was not a question when he said it.

"Fine, but what do you propose I do while you do that? Enter the possibly dangerous room with you or stay alone and vulnerable in the hallway?" she questioned sarcastically. Although she clearly meant it as a joke, his face grew confused as he seriously weighed the options.

"You are right, you will come in with me, at least if there is danger, I can protect you."

"Good choice, we better go then." Alveen did not wait for Jayuk to secure the room, she swung the doors open and entered. The room was still and darker than the deepest abyss. "See nothing to worry about." As she said it, she didn't even believe the words she spoke. Something felt eerie as she hesitantly stepped across her floor. Jayuk attempted to light her vanity, but he could not summon the magic he needed. A foul odor found its way to her, a rotten salty stench like that of rotten seaweed.

"Banphrionsa, I do not like the feeling of this." He reached for her arm through the darkness but could not find her. She was just standing right next to him. "Banphrionsa Alveen? This is not funny."

"Actually," a voice so deep that it rumbled his core spoke all the way from the balcony. The full moon illuminated the figure and the horrified Jayuk stumbled trying to search for Alveen. "I find it quite entertaining."

A syragon stood absorbing the moonlight. It's figure much like that of a centaur, only its lower body was almost reptilian, like a dragon. He could see the dull scales that lined its back down to the semi-translucent fin at the end of its tail, and its sharp webbed wings that folded flush against its flanks. Its upper body was that of a siren, though it seemed to be twice Jayuk's size when considering his bulk. It contradicted the lower half with smooth, algae covered skin paler than the moon itself with dreadlocks of seaweed and kelp dripping onto the concrete beneath the creature. It slowly turned its head to face Jayuk. Its jaw line protruded and the facial features were distinct. All of that was soon overlooked when it gave an unnatural grin, exposing the razor-sharp fangs that filled his mouth, and its eyes were barren white, unlike the solid black of a mermaid.

As it turned to face Jayuk he saw a limp Alveen in his arms. "What did you do to her?"

"I believe she fainted from fear." The syragon said unconvincingly. "Or I may have knocked her unconscious to make the fly back to my sorceress much easier." Its wings unfolded, and it gracelessly lifted above where it previously stood.

An evil smile crawled across Jayuk's face as the creature slowly flew away. "Give the sorceress my salutation. Tell her I will return home soon."

~Chapter X~

Permission to court

The restaurant was overflowing with joyous laughs and conversations as Samual entered. It took only a moment for his trained eyes to find his friend across the merriment. Cautiously he crossed the hardwood floor, being sure not to step in the paths of any of the fumbling creatures as he made his way back to the table at which Zakarian sat, sipping on a frothy infusion.

"I'll have one of those." Samual requested as he approached the table. Zakarian raised his hand gesturing for two more.

"They are quite delicious and will not leave us shuffling out the door." He laughed referring to the already intoxicated

● ● ●

fairies falling out the restaurant threshold. "It will be nice to spend time with you, Samual. Things have been much too serious, and I have many things I wish to discuss with you, being as close of a friend as you are to me."

"I agree, I have something I wish to speak with you about also." Samual had decided before he walked in here that there was no use in being nervous about it, especially to Zakarian whom he knew would be able to tell. "But by all means, your issues first." Their drinks, frothing over the rim of the metallic copper mugs, arrived steaming in front of their faces. The aroma of mint and lavender swirled through the air as Samual brought the mug to his lips.

"Was I right?" Zakarian questioned with a grin across his face. Samual shook his head.

"What is this?" he had never tasted anything this wonderful before.

"It is an infusion I requested be made. I am unsure what to call it, but our warlock friend promised that it would make us relax without making a fool of ourselves." They touched mugs as took another swill of the beverage.

"So, where shall we start?"

"First things first, let us move to the roof where there is less eavesdroppers." Samual had no argument with that. Zakarian nodded to the warlock behind the bar, who walked out and led them to the locked staircase. "Thank-you sir." The man nodded and went back to working as they ascended the steps only visible by the few sconces that hung on the wall.

Stepping onto the roof top, Samual kept his focus on the twirled together branches making up the roof they stood on exposed to the night sky. Zakarian leaned his back against one of the thick branches that shot up, slowly sinking down to the floor, mug still in hand. Samual's messy locks swayed in the night breeze as he ran a hand through the stubble that he had come to like on his face, though he made sure to keep it extremely short.

"Alright, first order of business. Do you remember Malika?"

"Yes! I have not seen her in some time. Though I hear she has a child now." He paused, unsure if his friend was aware that his childhood crush was a mother. "Is that what this is about?" Samual knew of their love connection before Zakarian left. Malika had become heartbroken and never left her home. One day she had a child. No one knew with whom, or when.

"Yes."

"I have no idea who is the father. I never even saw her pregnant. She just suddenly had a baby."

"It's me. I'm the father. Before I left we shared a romantic evening, and of it." He didn't finish his sentence.

"Honestly?" Samual questioned, but by the look on Zakarian's face, Samual could tell this was no joke, and may have been the reason for his relaxing elixir. The man was stressed. "Does anyone else know?"

"I informed Alveen. Though she has never met Malika, or the child, and she does not understand the sensitivity in the issue. I want to tell people, I want to be the father I should have been for this little girl all along." He tapped his finger on the metal mug, "Malika and I have been spending much time together since my return, I wish to make it official."

"Then why don't you? Your grandmother has always been against the relationship. It's not as if the whole thing would be a surprise. And that little girl is part elf, she deserves the higher respect and the chance to the throne. You and Alveen will not be around forever. She is your heir, whether your grandmother likes it or not." Samual felt a little better about what he had to ask knowing that Zakarian also had some news The Queen would not take lightly.

"You are right. I need to approach her soon and get things cleared up. My daughter deserves the life of respect." The mug met his lips again and the last of the drink was gone. Samual still had over half a mug left.

"What else is bothering you?"

"My mother." He spoke quiet this time.

"Do you think she's still alive?"

"I'm not sure. I want to believe she's alive, but I don't want to believe that she abandoned her people and family for those wretched tribes. I had always looked up to her."

"I remember that." He paused thinking of how technically no one had seen either of their parents die. "What about your father?"

"I have to believe he died in the fire. I have no proof telling me otherwise." Samual just nodded his head, not wanting to push too far on such a sensitive subject. "Speaking of family; I am normally very good at reading Alveen, but she is confusing me."

"How so?"

"I spent the evening with her, teaching her magic, which she has gotten much better at controlling, and trying to learn more about her opinion of this place. I can't shake this feeling that she is keeping secrets from me."

"Alveen looks up to you, why would she keep secrets from you? And what would they be about do you think?" Curiosity pushed through Samual's self control. Was it just him that she was keeping secret, or was there more?

"I suggested finding a suitor the other day. Since she is of age." Zakarian mumbled, "But she claims to me she has a suitor. Why would she keep that from me? Why would she not tell me the minute she thought she liked someone or someone had interest in her? I do not understand that girl. We've never had secrets." He was flustered and his eyebrows pushed together as he thought of his sisters actions.

"Did she tell you who?" Samual wanted know exactly what Alveen had told Zakarian before he revealed his part in it.

"No. I thought it was that guard I put with her, Jayuk. He seemed to be very interested in her, but she claims it is not him and she has no interest in him because he's rude and arrogant. I don't see that. She said she will tell me when she figures out if her and him are on the same page. As if they may be having issues or have not discussed it." He brought his mug up to his lips, and a disappointed look landed on his face when he realized it was still empty.

"That was actually what I wanted to talk to you about." Samual had no idea how to word his request.

"What? You know who it is?"

"Yes…and I know why she hasn't told you." Zakarian had jumped to his feet excited that he was finally going to be getting information.

"Zakarian. I would feel privileged, if you would give me your blessing to court Alveen." Zakarian stood still and gave him a disbelieving look.

"You?" He scoffed with a smile.

"Yes, is there something wrong with that?" Samual became defensive.

"I don't believe it. I would have noticed. Certainly, I would have noticed."

"It is true, I swear it. I spoke with her and we agreed we have the same direction in this relationship and wanted to pursue it further. And she informed me that it is proper etiquette to ask for permission to court The Princess, though I'm sure she knows I am already aware of this."

"I want to hear this from her lips. "Zakarian did not seem upset, but he seemed simply stunned. "Let's go find her ourselves, shall we?" He turned expecting Samual to stop him and admit it was merely a jest. Samual gestured for them to go and followed him down the stairs back into the loud establishment.

"Thank-you Sir. It was delicious. What do we owe?" Samual asked trying to pay the tab as Zakarian was still walking away.

"It's on the house. He looked like he'd been having a rough day."

"Thank-you" Samual bowed and walked out after his friend towards the palace nearby. Zakarian walked with confidence as if he was about to prove his friend wrong, but Samual had a 'you'll see' look glued to his face as he followed.

~Chapter XI~
Over his dead body

Her heart pounded as she came to her senses. Her arm slid across something that felt like algae or gel, and only moments she later realized why. A syragon, the creature she had always been told evil stories about, the creature that forced her to lose her memories, had finally come back to finish the job. She heard him speak, and she was so close to it that it shook her entire body, it's voice so deep that it was as if it was possessed.

"Give the sorceress my salutation. Tell her I will return home soon." Alveen opened her eyes to see an eerie grin plastered on Jayuk's face as he spoke. This was a set up. He knew this monster was waiting for her and purposely led her in. Her mind reeled trying to piece together some kind of plan. She could feel the height they gained as he slowly lifted higher off the balcony. She saw her arm begin to glow where it touched the creature that held her. She knew what that meant; Magic. She had never used it before, but this was the perfect time to use what little she knew. She focused all her energy on her hand that rested on the algae covered skin of the beast and soon she could feel the magic inside this creature transferring to her. The more magic built up inside her, the more desperately it screamed for an outlet. The beast suddenly had a difficult time keeping the height, its body being exhausted as it's source of life slowly drained.

"Over my dead body!" Alveen screamed as she slid from the grips of the abomination. She cried out as its talons pierced her skin and the ribs beneath as it reached for her tumbling to the floor. Her heart pounded as she protected her wounds with her hands, covering them in her warm blood. She was bleeding, it took her a few second to realize how much blood she was losing.

"Do not think you are stronger than me, foolish Banphrionsa. I know you do not remember much, but I thought we taught you a lesson already." It walked towards her with a powerful strut, its talons scraping against the stone floor she now crawled on. Turning onto her back she tried to remember what Zakarian had taught her. Elemental magic was going to take a lot less energy, and she assumed it took a lot to kill a creature of this size. She took a deep breath, slowly blew into her hands and bent her fingers as if she was holding a ball of wind. Her hands began to radiate light as she extended her arm. It was working. Alveen's emotions grew strong as she tried to defend herself, the magic screaming as she tried to release everything that was caged up inside her.

A repeated flash of heat and light exploded toward the creature, shaking the walls. Alveen slowly pushed herself to her feet, realizing it was coming from her, blinding and holding back both of her opponents. Alveen stood tall, a new confidence formed inside her and she used it to her advantage. Twisting her arms, she aimed towards the syragon. The creature bent down in pain, screeching as its fate was apparent. Alveen was engrossed in battle. She did not think of anything else. It came as a second nature to her, as she stood in the center of her room with a stern expression. She walked towards the syragon, collecting all the power she could in her palm, readying to defeat it. A laugh rang out behind her.

"Do you really believe you can kill both of us?" She looked to see her bodyguard transforming before her eyes, into a much smaller version of the monster that knelt before her. "You will die a painful, excruciating-" Alveen had heard enough, she spun around and forcefully extended her arm in his direction, sending him through her bed chamber door. She said nothing, her facial expression never changing.

"Alveen!" Zakarian and Samual stood at the door, seeing Alveen for the first time in nearly full power, her teal and golden eyes glowing much like her hands. "Alveen, you do not know how to control it. Relax." Samual checked the syragon lying in the shards of wood in the hall.

"She killed it." He said amazed. "Alveen, we're here now. Please, breathe, contract your power. I don't want you to hurt yourself."

She smiled, recognizing him and focusing on him instead of the magic that swelled up inside her. Only for a moment did she seem like herself, until she heard the groan of the original syragon who was slowly standing back on all fours. Her face grew serious and she clenched her fists. Samual would not be able to help her now.

Her battle cry rang through the palace as she flexed her arms by her sides, releasing all the pent-up magic that she had absorbed from the syragon across her room. Samual pulled Zakarian to the outside of the wall, protecting them from the intense heat that was radiating off Alveen. The syragon was incinerated before her eyes, and the final bit of magic left her body, making her collapse to her hands and knees.

"Alveen?" Samual whispered as he peeked out from around the wall and started towards the bent over girl in the center of the room. As he approached her he noticed her shoulders and feet were bare. She had literally incinerated her clothes, everything except the cloak, which is made to withstand magic. "Let's cover you up." He knelt behind her grabbing the edges of the cloak about to toss them forward for her to cover herself, when he noticed her shoulders and arms were covered in burns. She had deep steady breathes, but through the burns on her cheeks, forehead and neck he could see she was using her last bit of strength to hold back crying. "Alveen?"

"Don't touch me. Please." She was in an excruciating amount of pain.

"Alveen we need to get you to the healers immediately."

"No. Bring them here. I cannot move." She spoke through soft cries, trying to put on a show as if she was unaffected. As the tears began to leave her eyes, she clenched as they burned trailing over her exposed wounds.

"Zakarian! Get the healers. NOW." Samual commanded him. The potion he drank was only just starting to wear off. He ran, yelling for the guards to search the city for more intruders, inspect how they would have gotten in undetected and fetch the healers.

"Tell them there is nothing more important right now." Zakarian ordered.

"Samual?" She whispered as he knelt in front of her, covering her bare skin.

"Yes love?"

"Don't leave me. Please don't leave me alone." He wanted so desperately to hold onto her and promise she would never be alone again, but he knew doing so would cause her physical pain. He sat with her in silence until the healer arrived.

"I need her to stand up." Leigheas told Samual as she walked in.

"Keep everyone out of here!" Samual shouted to the guards. "Prince Zakarian and Banri Vailion are the only ones allowed to pass." He stood ordering different guards around then turned back to her.

"Samual I need her to move, I cannot treat her unless she is exposed."

"Can we move her to the bathroom? I think she deserves that much respect She has no clothes other than her cloak." Leigheas agreed kneeling down to address The Princess. "Samual is going to move you Princess Alveen. We won't touch you, but keep breathing deep okay?" She explained. He stepped back and extended his hands, palms up as he carefully levitated her off the ground, leaving her with her back facing the approaching crowd. He slowly stepped towards the bathroom in her room and lowered her down onto the spongy moss.

"Thank-you Samual."

"Alveen, I'm going to be right outside the door." She shook her head enough to acknowledge that she heard him. They had hardly even begun courting, it would be far too inappropriate if he saw her undressed. Moments later The Banri emerged from the crowd of guards and palace staff.

"What happened here!?" The Banri demanded, furious as she approached Samual. "Why is my grandson tending to a dead syragon in my palace hallway? How did this happen?"

"We have guards looking into it. Zakarian and I approached The Princess's room, only to be greeted by Princess Alveen somehow coming into an extreme amount of magic able to throw a syragon through the solid palace door." The Banri stood shocked. "And she continued to use this magic until it had somehow been extinguished, incinerating another, quite large syragon, who is now there." He pointed towards the large pile of ashes. The Banri's jaw dropped as she looked around the room.

"How did she do this? She has had hardly enough training to execute such a feat."

"Apparently training isn't what she needed."

"Where is she?"

"She is in the bathroom with Leigheas."

"Why is Leigheas here? What happened to my granddaughter?" She demanded, heading towards the door.

"My Banri, please. She is in extremely rough shape right now. Her body is covered in burns and she can hardly move or talk." The Queen hesitated, she opened the door and her face dropped as she saw her granddaughter.

"Maybe I shall wait out here until Leigheas is finished with her work." Samual nodded his agreement.

~CHAPTER XII~

HEALING

Zakarian had taken care of the syragon bodies and the crowd had dispersed by the time Leigheas emerged from the bathroom. A few staff members surveyed the damage, preparing for the remodel of her chamber.

"She will heal. She is exhausted, and she doesn't look the same, yet." She spoke soft.

"What do you mean yet?" The Banri asked.

"She suffered severe burns, I have done everything I can at this time to heal her wounds. She has potions to take daily and she will need a daily visit from me, so I can perform more healing on her in order to return her skin to its normal state."

"As long as she is alive and recovering, we are grateful. Thank-you for coming so quickly." Samual bowed to her.

"And as always, royal business is to be discreet. No one will know of exactly what happened here" The Banri stated as Leigheas walked out. Samual entered the bathroom first to see Alveen bent over the toilet.

"Apparently healing causes you to be quite nauseous." She sarcastically pointed out. He walked up, about to rub her back. "Please don't. It is healing but it does still hurt. Thankfully not nearly as bad." Retreating his hand, he stood by her, realizing he had yet to speak to The Banri about courting The Princess and now was not that time.

"We are just grateful you are alive. What happened?" The Banri questioned immediately.

"If you are ready to talk about it." Samual quickly added.

"Of course, I'm doing much better. Leigheas actually made me a drink so I fell asleep while she performed her healing." Alveen turned around facing them, leaning against the cold stone wall. She didn't look much different than before. Leigheas had performed her duty flawlessly as always. Alveen's arms were covered in scars but her face seemed to have aged a little, though the impact healing has probably made her even more exhausted. "So, Jayuk was a syragon. Not quite sure how that got by us." She started.

"Um, What?" Zakarian said, offended at the thought that he would have put his sister in danger.

"Yep. When I returned to my chambers, the door was slightly open. I thought maybe Mysti was here. Jayuk led me in and then I'm not sure what happened. When I woke back up I was in that monster's arms and I heard Jayuk say something about telling the sorceress he would be home soon."

"You managed to escape the grips of a syragon?" The Banri questioned, impressively.

"Yes." She paused feeling her rib cage. Leigheas was an astonishing healer, and her broken bones were mended at least, but she still felt the deep scars under her borrowed shirt. "I wasn't sure how it happened, but my arm was leaning against its skin and started to glow, but it looked like in was in my veins, flowing through me. When I came to my senses and saw what danger I was in, I slid out of its arms, but not without this." She paused and lifted the shirt Leigheas gave her. Across her stomach and ribs were four deep wounds that were now sickening scars. "She healed the broken bones, so I'm lucky this is all that's left. Anyways, I tried to remember things I had read and the little Zakarian had explained to me, and I somehow managed to control wind, and after that there was so much pent up power inside me from whatever happened when I touched the syragon, that I just let go. I didn't lose control, by the way, that was intentional." She aimed the last remark at her brother. "I just dropped the wall. I wanted all of it out and I knew it was going to take just that." They all stared at her. "And that's what happened."

"You realize you are one of the only people to be able to control that much magic, don't you?" Samual commented, breaking the silence.

"No." she paused taking that in, "I thought it was something anyone could do."

"We wouldn't have nearly as much of a problem with them if we could do that."

"Oh, so why am I so different? Why was I able to do that?" She hadn't realized the significance. "What does this mean?" She asked as she adjusted herself against the corner of the wall.

"I... I'm not sure. We will most certainly be looking into it though." The Banri stated, puzzled by the facts laid out before her.

"It means we need to start your training. Serious training." Zakarian replied and then focused towards the Banri and Samual. "I think once she is healed she needs to start training, both with me and Samual." Alveen closed her eyes and let out a breath.

"Keep me updated on any information you find out about how those creatures got in the castle and how they even managed to come on land. Also, when she is fully healed I would like to be informed as well. In the meantime, I am giving you both a set of guards.

"Yes, Grandmother." Zakarian answered as she exited the bathroom, then spoke to Samual. "We should let Alveen rest. I will move her to my bed." Palm up, Zakarian summoned magic and without touching her, he moved Alveen to his chambers. Samual followed with silent footfalls behind them down the hallway, through all the arched doorways and vines manipulated into looking like intricate detail among the walls leading to Zakarian's wing of the palace.

Samual opened the door expecting a much more lavish suite than it would appear The Prince had. Vines draped over the walls of exposed stone, the floor was all large flat stepping stones of various neutral colors with moss growing between everyone. His bed frame was constructed of trees growing directly from the floor creating a four-post bed and canopy which sat directly across from an elaborate mantel created from the leafless entwined branches and vines. The flames were shoulder high contained in the hearth of the fireplace, and directly across from the door they entered was a curved wall of arched windows that looked out over Cosaint. You could see everything from here. Samual took everything in as he always did when he entered a new place.

Zakarian lowered Alveen after Samual pulled back the lightweight covers and gently laid them over her. He wanted to lean down and kiss her but he wasn't sure how well her skin healed.

"Would you like to stay with her first?" Zakarian asked.

"I shouldn't. I need to go interview and prep new guards for you both, Your Highness. Seeing as we had one betray us obviously for some time, it seems some investigating must begin." He stared at his Princess's face for a moment longer, "Please let me know if you need me and when she wakes."

He decided to head home for the evening, it was late, and The Queen surely would not appreciate a political call at this hour. Exiting the palace, he headed towards the bay to the tree he called home. Pulling himself onto the graciously constructed porch that wrapped around the one-bedroom home he unclasped his cloak, hanging it outside the entrance doorway. He exhaled vocally as he entered the large room. It wasn't a palace room, but it was home. Along an entire wall was his kitchen, with windows opening to the bay below. He headed towards the back door, passing the premade bed that sat diagonally in the corner of the room, where a shower awaited outside, three walls to give privacy. The porch floor he stood on matched the stained planks that ran across the interior. Wrapping a towel around himself he fell back on his bed, too awake to sleep. After putting a pair of plaid pajama pants on, he sat in the chair by his small fireplace. It was not shoulder high, but it warmed the place as needed. There were no flames now, as he was enjoying the now crisp breeze that came with the season change. He sat, thinking of how he could protect The Princess. He would speak with The Banri first thing in the morning, which would probably be the best time to address his intentions with Alveen. He sighed, resting his face in his palms.

Morning came and Samual stood, he waved his hand in the air in front of him, summoning Zakarian. A cloud appeared before him, Zakarian's face sleepy.

"Good Morning Prince. How is The Princess?" He directly asked.

"She is still sleeping. Though she has been rustling so I expect she will be awake soon."

"I will stop by and relieve you once I have spoken with The Banri this morning."

"I'm still asking Alveen about our conversation." He mentioned with a smile as if saying 'don't think I forgot'. Samual shook his head with a smile and waved his hand opposite, dissolving the fog ending their conversation.

Samual was out the door immediately after he had eaten, heading to the throne room to address The Queen on her wishes to sort out any possible betrayals in the midst of his order. He passed multiple staff members on his way hardly paying them any attention as he approached the golden doors. Guards were stationed outside standing tall. In their grips were double edged axes that stood as tall as the centaurs gripping them. The staff the blades were attached to had vines wrapped around, glowing a soft bioluminescence in the shadows of the hall.

"Head of Palace Guard approaches Your Majesty." One of the men said. The golden doors swung open, revealing the pillars of tree trucks and stone covered floor leading to the beautiful Queen standing in a plain black strapless gown, her straight dark locks of hair hung to the center of her shoulder blades and supported a glittering diamond circular crown.

"Banri, I come to strategize with you in regard to choosing the proper protection for The Prince and Princess."

"I'm glad to hear this Samual, as it seems our first choice was not a wise one."

"We must come up with a plan to weed out any others that may be in league with the Dorcha tribes. I fear this is only the beginning of whatever revolution they think they are planning." The Queen nodded in agreement, pacing in thought. Samual had a few ideas but none which he was sure would work.

"I know I can trust you Samual so I order you to be on duty for both of them, whether that means half days with each or however you may choose. But you will notice any unacceptable behavior and hopefully neither of them will have to nearly kill themselves defending their own lives if someone else is there." Samual paused before answering. "Is that a problem?" She stopped and stared at him, her peridot eyes digging into him.

"Not a problem but I do wish to be honest with you My Banri. Prince Zakarian has recently given me his blessing to court Princess Alveen, before all of this happened. I do wish to pursue that as well, but I wanted you to be aware of the depth of relationship." She was silent, but she looked at him with respect. His heart was beating rapidly with the suspense of how she would react.

"I appreciate you being honest with me, it seems to be something that comes rarely in our time now. However, I do not feel that this causes issue at this current time, if anything it will give you more incentive to do this job well as you have feelings for her." Samual's heart relaxed. "However, this will be your only warning. If you distract her from her duties or training, you will answer for it, and if it becomes too much of a distraction being around her, I will remove you from your assignment." She had a stern expression "And Samual, I respect you." She walked forward with a tone that insisted that she had more to say, "But if you disrespect my granddaughter, Your Princess, in any way, you will lose much more than just your title." Samual nodded in understanding with a smile on his face getting approval from The Queen. She continued "And realize that as Banphrionsa she has responsibilities to her kingdom. As you were honest with me, I will be bluntly honest with you, More than one gentleman may try to win her affection, and should a better match come along, take no offense, but I will encourage it, though it is ultimately up to her." That was a sting to his ego, should a better match come along? He chose to ignore the comment, he was fully aware that anyone would be allowed to win her affections, she was not closed off to the world until she was engaged. It did bring a tinge of jealousy to his chest as he thought back to how he felt when he thought Jayuk was trying to win her over, when he thought she was encouraging his flirtations. But after the recent episode, he realized how important she was, and how unique this royal was going to be. Of course others would try to win her heart, why wouldn't they?

"May I ask, how far is The Princess in her training?" He was going to do his best work, feelings aside, she was The Princess and she had duties, he of all people understood this.

"She is almost finished with her cultural lessons, she must still learn royal interactions." She clasped her hands together letting out a sigh, "Which is horrible timing, but I am glad you are here, because I have decided we must have a royal walk. As discrete as I try to keep things, it's only a matter of days before all of Beannaithe will hear of the attack on our recently returned Princess, which I have also tried to keep quiet. I understand your time with her, along with the training of Ollamh Hilfyro, she has been in the village and has yet to offend someone or act indecently so I do not fear any mishaps. She seems to be fitting in rather well." As she walked back to the throne she added more "And our ally royals will be here to participate as usual. So be prepared and see to the arrangements for our guests. I have confirmation of four kingdoms." Samual raised an eyebrow, there were six kingdoms total, was there one refusing to show.

"Only four, Your Majesty?"

"I have yet to receive word from Bulgrakta. King Luka is much like his father was and prefers to not answer to anyone, so he may surprise us and show up unannounced." Samual nodded understanding. The new King of Bulgrakta was said to be rude, silent and from what he heard, immensely intimidating. He pushed aside the gossip he heard and turned back to addressing Alveen.

"She has always been as intelligent as she is beautiful. I shall see to it that it is worked into her schedule and I shall place instructions, so chambers are ready in the guest wing for our visitors." He bowed as The Queen stood with her hands clasped in front of her and he departed the throne room.

"Caspian." He called to a guard walking towards him, "What news do you have for me?" The white centaur's hooves clicked on the stone. He towered over Samual. He was lower in rank, and Samual had no issue with feeling confident around his warriors. His shoulder-length platinum blonde hair was pulled into a ponytail at the nape of his neck. His eyes green like the leaves stared down at Samual with frustration.

"We did a sweep of our warriors, looking through their homes and the compound. It seems the sorceress had eyes in multiple locations. We have only found one other staff member who refuses to talk and seems to be in direct contact with her, but we have successfully removed all the crystal balls she had placed around town to spy. Multiple citizens were reporting back to her."

"So, it is worse than we feared. She is infiltrating the tribe already. The village will soon be in panic if we do not address this, but this may be the perfect time for a display of the

* * *

monarchy. The Queen wishes to have a royal walk for Alveen. The citizens will need that confirmation. I am going to her now and I will speak to Zakarian. Gather up a group of fifteen of our most trustworthy warriors. I do not have time or patience for another assassination attempt." He stormed off to Zakariam's wing of the palace, Caspian bowed in obedience.

Zakarian was watching over his sister when his solid chamber door echoed. He wasn't sure who he would be expecting. He confidently walked to the door, prepared to defend himself if necessary, but thinking logically, what enemy would knock on his door? The door moved open slowly and fingers wrapped around the edge lower on the door than to be expected. As he approached, the intruder poked her head around for him to see her glowing pink irises. "Tanilly, what are you doing here? Where is your mother?" The little girl jumped at the sound of his voice, startled.

"She said she was looking for you."

"She left you alone? How did you know where my chamber was in the first place?" He didn't mean to overwhelm her but she started breathing heavy with all his questions, as if she were scared.

"Um, no.. well. . . yes, she left me alone outside the play room. I was supposed to go in, but I wanted to help her find you. One of the people in the hallway told me where to find you." He wanted to be irritated and to scold her for entering without being welcomed in, but she was just a child.

"Let's go find your mom. Give me just a moment, alright?" she shook her head in understanding as Zakarian walked to the window waving his hand in front of him summoning

Samual. A fog began to form in front of him and an image of Samual appeared.

"It's only been a couple hours, miss me already?" He was smiling.

"I seem to have something I need to take care of, can you be here soon to continue guard?" Samual nodded acknowledging he was on his way. A small gasp came from across the room when the fog disappeared.

"Is that The Princess? Is she okay?" Tanilly approached the bed slowly.

"Yes," Zakarian quickly stood in her way. "It is The Princess. Now go sit by the window while I summon you mother." She listened. Zakarian walked into the hallway as he thought there may be a few choice words they needed to have. She sat on the window sill staring at Alveen. She admired her blonde curls that lay messy on the pillow and couldn't help but get closer to her. She felt a pull to her, involuntarily moving her towards the towering bed frame.

The door flew open and Samual quickly came in.

"Oh." He said once he noticed the little girl near the bed. "Who are you?" She stood frozen. She recognized him, but he intimidated her.

"This is Tanilly. Malika seems to have misplaced her daughter. I need to go find her as she is not answering when I summon her." Samual's gaze went back and forth between the young girl and the Prince, he knew this was his daughter, but he knew she did not know this yet.

* * *

"Oh, my apologies. I will let you two be on your way then." They closed the door behind them and Samual paced the room. He stood at the window and admired the village he protected for a long while.

"See anything you like?" He heard from behind him as the sun began to rise into the sky. The voice made his heart race as he turned around to see The Princess sitting up adjusting pillows behind her back.

"Nothing that compares to what I see now" His eyes softened as he looked at her, his serious appearance faded when he looked at her. He melted around her. "I've missed you" he smiled walking towards her. "How are you feeling?"

"Surprisingly, I feel well. A little weak, but well." She was staring down at her hands. "And I missed you too." He couldn't wait. He rushed to her side, placing a hand behind her head and one arm around her waist. She tensed for a second before she gave into his embrace. He rested his forehead on hers.

"My sweet Princess," He brought his lips to meet hers briefly then rested her head on his shoulder as he embraced her. "You don't know how much I have needed this." She was silent for a moment as she traced her fingers down his back.

"Samual?" He sat up looking into her eyes, holding her hands.

"Yes love?"

"Where am I?" She laughed a little taking in her surroundings. She had never been in this room before.

"This is Zakarian's room. Yours needs a little..."

"Work? Needs to be completely rebuilt?" She smiled. "How did I do that anyways?" He thought for a second.

"I honestly have no idea. You have learned very little about control, but the magic in you must have been growing for so long it finally found its release. I'm just grateful you were able to be healed." She looked down at herself, hand over her gruesome scars as if she were standing in front of the beasts again, covering the freshly made wound. She snapped back to reality realizing she was not in her clothes.

"Any chance any of my clothes survived?" She asked wanting to shower and change.

"Possibly, but I'm sure your grandmother is on top of that already." He paused, he wanted to wait to tell her but he was too excited, "Speaking of her and Zakarian.." he trailed off.

"Yes?" Her eyes lit up a little, but he wasn't sure that she was certain what he was going to say.

"I spoke with them. About us." He tried not to sound too excited to keep the suspense.

"Oh my gosh, tell me! What happened?" He smiled at her impatience.

"We're good. Well, Zakarian still believes I was fooling him and that this is not a reality, so he plans to talk to you about it. The Banri was actually supportive, I expected more of a struggle from her, but she is putting me in charge of your personal guard, as she is assuming my feelings for you will make me that much more certain that you are protected at any cost." He didn't even have a moment to breathe until her lips were on his and her arms around his neck pulling him closer, before he even knew she understood what he told her.

"I'm really happy we didn't have to be rebels just to be together. But just know I would have done it, for you." She smiled laying her head on his chest. Then she sat up suddenly. "Wait, what do you mean my guard?"

"She is ordering you and Zakarian your own private guard to ensure you are defended if there is another assassination attempt, or kidnapping attempt. But I will be with you most of the time now. Caspian, my second in command, will be taking over training for a while. And we need to get you training right away. Also, your grandmother orders a royal walk, which is just you get all fancy to confidently strut around the village to ensure them that you're courageous and that the attack did not waiver the monarchy. They need to know they have strong rulers." She nodded, it must have made sense to her because she didn't question it.

"When will this walk take place? What do I need to do?"

"Probably tomorrow. Essentially nothing out of the ordinary, you will need to use proper etiquette and formal titles, so you will address me as Head Guard or Sir Samual. The village will have music and dancing and will celebrate the strength of their rulers."

"Sounds like fun." She pulled the covers off herself and her gaze landed on her dirty v neck shirt and leggings the healer had given her. "Will you ask The Queen if there are any clothing options I have, even if it's just another set of these clothes? I must shower."

. . .

"Are you okay to do that? I mean your skin." He trailed off not sure how to address that. "Doesn't it still hurt? Leigheas will be here soon. She said you require another treatment. Do you think possibly it would be better to wait?"

"Only slightly. I don't think a shower will hurt badly. I am laying here just fine." She got to her feet and slowly walked around the room, admiring the craftsmanship of the chamber until her eyes stopped at the flames in the fireplace. She stood in front of it, letting the warmth envelope her as she gazed into it folding her arms across her chest. "But you are probably right, another healing wouldn't hurt." Her face still looked worn and exhausted and he hadn't noticed until now but down across her temple to her cheek bone on one side was an indent from the burn that was recently there.

Samual moved slowly behind her, staring into the same flames. He reached up resting one hand on her bicep and another on her opposite hip as he leaned forward and rested his head on her shoulder. He felt her exhale deeply as she relaxed in his hold. Her eyes met his, but she said nothing. The teal color he so desired reflected the dancing flames in the hearth as if he could see her passion as she stared at him with a grateful gaze. She admired his features that the shadows enhanced. His sharp jaw line decorated with the faint facial hair growing in, his eyes a dark brown that nearly blended with his pupils made her melt under the heat of his gaze. She nuzzled into his chest and relaxed, grateful to feel his touch after the fear that it would be much longer before she could have physical contact with anyone considering her injuries.

● ● ●

~Chapter XIII~
Royal introductions

It killed Zakarian that Tanilly did not know of their relationship yet, but he would still protect her and embrace the time he had with her. He carried the young girl through the palace and saw no sign of Malika. He searched the streets of the villages, the training grounds and asked some of the fairies if they had seen her, no one knew where she was. He began to get worried as the sun began to slowly descend from the sky.

"Are we going to find my mommy?" Her eyes began to glow as tears ran down her cheeks. It broke his heart. He had guards out looking for his love now that he had done a quick search himself.

● ● ●

"Yes, my dear, I have many people looking for her. Why don't we go eat dinner?" She shook her head and rested against his shoulder in his arms as he carried her back to the palace.

As he approached the palace ramp a hooded figure appeared from the shadows. The guards saw the intruder only moments before he did and in swift quick movements managed to grab hold. "Guards! Who is sneaking around the palace so late?" Zakarian called. The first guard pulled the hood back to reveal the familiar pink eyes of the woman he loved. "Malika? Why are you disguised? You know you are welcome to the palace, especially to get your child." The last sentence had a tone reminding her that she even had a child.

"Zakarian! Oh, Thank Solas! I wasn't sneaking around. The air is crisp tonight. Am I not allowed to wear a hood to cover myself from the cold?" She pulled away from the guards. "Why do you have her out here?" She began frantically.

"She actually came to my chambers. Said her mother was looking for me."

"I dropped her off at the child care wing."

"She never went in. Someone in the palace told her where I was, and she managed to get to my wing of the palace by herself. We have been searching for you. Why didn't you answer my summons?" He asked her innocently.

"You never went into the classroom? Tanilly, you must start listening. You could have been hurt or lost or worse. Do not ever do that again, do you hear me young fairy?" Tanilly shook her head, still in Zakarians arm as Malika reached for her. "Thank-you for keeping an eye on her Zakarian. I'm sure she enjoyed the time she spent with you." And with that she walked off towards their home, never answering Zakarian's concerns. He ordered the guards back to their posts as he walked inside the palace for the night, speechless at the peculiar conversation.

"Finally back I see." The Banri stood in front of him not far from the throne room as he walked by to go to his wing of the palace. She was not asking questions. He bowed waiting for whatever she had to say. "Take these to your sister please. Some of her gowns were able to be salvaged from the blast, however many were destroyed. Here are some clothes for her for right now, and in the morning her gown for the walk will be available."

"Much appreciated Your Majesty. Any idea how long her chamber will take to repair?" He asked out of curiosity.

"Should only be another day before the fairies finish their work restoring it. Many things had to be remodeled so it is taking a little longer." With that she turned walking to the throne room with her gown trailing behind her as she disappeared through the closing golden doors.

Alveen slept on Samual's chest, him sound asleep as well, when Zakarian entered the room again. Maybe Samual was telling the truth. As the thought entered his mind, Samual's eyes flung open as the sound of the door swinging ajar entered his trained ears. Zakarian walked over toward his bathroom and hung Alveen's outfit up so she could clean up before he stepped into the cloud of warmth emitting from the fireplace. He glanced back at the two on his bed. He felt as if it should be bothering him, like it was inappropriate, but he was there as a chaperone per-say, and as odd as it seems having his best friend courting his younger sister, deep down he had a hunch all along that Samual's protective nature was like that of a devoted loved one. Though as he began to think, the duty to her would be rather similar to that of a husband, in the protective aspect anyways, needing to be fiercely loyal to her and her kingdom and watching out for any dangers that may threaten to steal her away. He would be good to her.

He still had not spoken to Alveen about the situation. He had his own relationships to worry about. It still puzzled him that Malika was so calm about her daughter roaming the village, even if it was with him.

He was now in his night clothes which consisted of a silk buttoned up shirt, a darker shade of black than the current nights sky which was elegantly splashed with bright stars, and matching silk pants tailored perfectly for his lean figure. Softly, he stepped over to his closet grabbing extra pillows and blankets, so he could take the couch this night in order to avoid waking Alveen.

"How has she been?" He asked the guard who still lay on the side of the bed, one of his legs touching the floor.

"Well. No more pain. Leigheas was here this morning and said her body took to the healing much better than she thought. She will have one more healing tomorrow morning. Her scars are smooth now, but still visible, and the skin on her face is back to normal." He ran a finger across where her scar ran earlier this morning.

"Samual, I apologize for not believing you. It seems odd. And I suppose I am hurt that she didn't tell me sooner." He stared at his friend, who was fawning over The Princess beside him. "I know you are well aware of this, but others will try to court her. You will be fighting for her affection Samual." He warned him, he knew his friend was the jealous type.

"I'm aware. But I have faith that we will prevail." Zakarian drifted off on the firm, hardly worn cloth sofa. Zakarian's head ran wild with thought of Malika and Tanilly.

Samual rose with the sun behind the mountains, slipping out of under Alveen's grip. He noticed Zakarian stretched out on the couch across the room. He glanced between Alveen and Zakarian and thought of how shocked his friend must have been when he entered his own chambers the night before. He didn't say anything to them, allowing them to relax and rest before the big day that lay ahead. Samual couldn't help but think something would get in the way of them being together, everything just seemed too easy. But for now, he would be grateful and enjoy the time they had and if conflict arises, they would conquer that together. There was a soft knock on the door. Assertively Samual strode across the floor, opening the solid door enough to see The Banri's guard.

"Ah, Sir Magnus, how may I be of assistance this morning?" The guard extended a rolled-up scroll with a teal ribbon tied around it.

"This is the Banphrionsa's schedule today. It will consist of greeting a few royals from nearby kingdoms who wish to be a part of the festivities today and show support. There will be a brunch feast, a late luncheon with the nobles of Cosaint, and then the royal walk will ensue, leading to the dinner feast. Then she is to return here and prepare for the ball, which will begin at nightfall at the training grounds. I was also informed that

Leigheas will be here shortly to do a physical exam of the Banphrionsa to ensure she is healing properly."

"Perfect, Thank-you Sir. I will ensure she is on time to every event." Sir Magnus bowed as he retreated towards the main area of the palace. When Samual opened the scroll. He was pleased to see they still had almost two hours until the other royals would be arriving, giving Alveen time to get ready and have her exam.

"That sounds like a day full, though I shouldn't be surprised." Zakarian sat up on the couch, having overheard the orders from Sir Magnus. "I am surprised we were not given a further notice for visitors though. I wonder who will be joining us today." His eyes quizzical as he thought about the nearby kingdoms.

"Wait, I'm going to be meeting other royals?" Alveen spoke, slowly pushing herself up on the bed, wrapping her arms around her knees as she leaned forward with interest, her eyes still tired.

"Yes. As far as we know there are four kingdoms royals visiting. I'm sure you've learned of the boarders and how the sorceress's minions live in the valleys. There are few boarders that are safe to cross without needing to cross over their lands. These royals are allies of ours though," Zakarian explained as he went to ready himself for the day of festivities.

"Are their kingdoms like ours? Ruled similar also?"

"Yes, pure elven monarchs across all six kingdoms. Some have slightly different climates being from different areas of our world. But I am sure you will learn that soon enough."

"Wait, I don't know how to interact with them. I should have been learning about the other kingdoms and how to be a proper diplomat. I'm going to look like a fool today!" Alveen began to worry. The weight of the crown was obvious to her this morning and she hadn't even stepped out of bed.

"Ollamh will get there. You still have many courses left. I will go over some simple rules, but since we are the hosting kingdom, it will be more prominent that they follow our customs, which you already know." This calmed her heart slightly. "Leigheas will be here soon, she wanted to do a final physical exam to see if there was any permanent damage." He stepped out of his closet as he spoke. He wore a burgundy and gold uniform, much like what she was used to seeing in regard to military before. Golden embroidery floated along his velvet sleeves leading to a large metal clasp at his shoulder from which hung a large brown and grey fur cape that hung to the back of his knees. "I will be prepping our guards for the day if Sir Magnus has not done so already. Your first outfit for today is hanging up. I will send for Mysti." With that he walked out the solid decorative door, leaving Samual and Alveen again.

"First outfit? Where did the clothes come from? How many times must I change today?" She questioned entering her brother's large expanse of a closet.

"You should have only two outfits, your first for introductions, brunch and the walk, and your second will be for the ball."

"A ball?" She must not have been given the entire schedule for she had never heard that today would be so demanding. "Am I okay to dress before Leigheas arrives?"

"Yes, her exam will be more magical. And yes, it will be held on the training grounds clearing. It shows your kingdom that you will always meet them where they are at and that you value their space as much as your own." His voice echoed as he still stood outside the closet giving her privacy to dress. "Your gown should match your brother's attire." Alveen was grateful for his comment as she was unsure which outfit was the first. Her fingers trailed along the matching burgundy gown, admiring it. The satin skirt was drizzled with golden embroidery of leaves and vines that danced up to the velvet bodice in a way that made it look as if a gorgeous figure already wore it, though it simply hung on the hanger. The sweetheart neckline would have been immodest had it not been for the illusion neckline, the sheer material covered in the continuing vines that sat where a necklace normally would. The gown had long sheer sleeves, allowing the vines to wrap and drape around where her biceps and forearms would go, and hanging near was a fur wrap, closely matching in color to the cape her brother wore.

"Banphrionsa, do you need assistance?" Mysti's voice surprised her.

"Yes please." She snapped out of her cloud of admiration and stepped out of her borrowed clothes and into the intricate gown, feeling the jersey like liner slide over her smooth legs and sliding her arms through the sheer material. "This is perfect. What is the significance of the colors Mysti? Zakarian and I are matching." Mysti looked only slightly shocked before explaining.

"These are your kingdoms colors, Your Highness. And today will be the change of season for us, so you will get to see the true beauty of where the kingdoms colors come from."

"I feel like a fool. All these things I never really thought about; other kingdoms, change in seasons. I suppose I had just expected it to be green and lush all year round."

"On the contrary, Your Highness. Your kingdom sees the most drastic season changes, some of the other kingdoms have less drastic changes, or hardly no changes at all." It made sense. Why wouldn't there be any sort of season change, though the magic here would make it possible she expected. Mysti twirled Alveen's hair, leaving it long to hang down her back and spent some time on her face to make her presentable to other royals. When she finished, she carefully wrapped Alveen's shoulders in the fur hung up and connected the large golden clasp at the front. Her wrap covered her chest, upper arms and upper back. "If you don't mind, Your Highness?" Mysti glanced over to the ornamental box encasing her jewelry and tiara already chosen for her today.

"Yes, of course" Mysti concentrated on the curls in front of her, deciding how to best place the tall diadem. "Here are your shoes, Your Highness." Alveen stood up and stepped into the satin deep red colored heels, with the perfectly matching leaves whimsically stretched along the side.

"Is there a mirror here?" Mysti waved her hand revealing a reflective cloud that formed in front of her, allowing Alveen to see herself before she stepped out into the room. She was speechless; never would she have thought she could look so regal. The crown Mysti chose stood tall atop her loose curls and elegantly braided bangs pinned back out of her face, with many peaks and valleys in it height, solid gold covered in scrolled embossing and engravings, and in her ears hung large golden leaves. Her face was decorated with golden and brown glittered shadow and a nude colored gloss shined on her lips. She looked magnificent and she felt like a true Princess.

"I believe Leigheas is here to do your final exam before you greet the royals." As Alveen stepped out of Zakarian's closet, she expected to see Samual, who stood at the far window, hands folded behind his back, standing as a true warrior. However, she was not expecting five other guards who she had never seen before. They stood sporadic throughout the room and Leigheas sat on the couch Zakarian had been on that morning with her bag contents sprawled across the table in an organized fashion.

"Oh, Your Highness!" She gasped. "You are simply glowing." Alveen glanced around the room, noticing admiration from every face she saw. Smiles played across the lips of a few guards and when her eyes met Samuals, his face gave way from his stoic mask and melted into pure admiration as he took in every detail in front of him. She pushed her shoulders back, stepping into her role.

"Thank-you, Leigheas. I feel a bit more put together than I was expecting." She gestured for Alveen to sit next to her.

"The royals will be ecstatic to finally meet you." She reached down and began making a small potion. "I do not wish to take up too much of your time since I know you have a busy day ahead of you, so this will be simple. Drink this" She handed Alveen a small glass of a green juice. "It will allow me to see ailments in your body by simply waving the wand over you, much less invasive than anything else."

"Do they all need to be here for this?" Alveen looked around the room at all the tough faces. She did not know these men and defiantly did not trust them yet enough for any ailments of The Princess's to be disclosed to them. Samual caught her meaning immediately.

"We will be waiting outside, Your Highness. We will escort you to the entrance when you are ready." He put on a professional face, leading the guards out of the chamber.

"Please stand." She aimed at The Princess. She followed instruction hoping to get this over with. Leigheas stood in front of her and picked up a solid white wand that lay on the table in front of her, swirled it in the air a few times and slowly waved it over Alveen's figure. She felt a cold chill run through her, but it was not painful. Her healer's face went pale staring at The Princess. "Your Highness, please lay down. It seems there may be something going on, but I would like to try to address it, before I come to any solid conclusions, if you don't mind." She guided her to the couch helping her lay down without ruining her outfit. Waving the white wand over her figure, she quietly chanted a few incantations before requesting that they do the test again. Alveen stood after the second glass of green juice was finished. Repeating the process, Leigheas's face showed the same emotion. "Your Highness, I fear there was damage I am unable to reverse with my current elixirs and spells." Hesitantly she asked,

"What exactly is irreversible?" Alveen's chest tightened, preparing for whatever was about to be thrown her way.

"I'm sorry, but it appears as though you will be unable to have children." Alveen stood silent standing across from her trusted healer. She had never thought about kids. Now was not the time to get distraught about it, she had too much on her mind. She would have time after the walk to digest the new information.

"Thank-you Leigheas, you have been most helpful." She gave her a glance of sympathy as she packed her bag and headed out the door. Alveen's stomach twisted with the thought of never being able to have an heir.

Samual entered as she exited, "Is everything alright Princess?" His tone was professional, but she knew it was meant to be personal since he did not use his native tongue. She stood tall and turned to face him, smoothing out the satin material and putting a smile on her face.

"Yes, everything is fine. Let's get on with our day." She clasped her hands together in front of her abdomen and glided out of the room, her guards falling into place around her, Samual at her side.

~CHAPTER XIV~
THE ROYAL WALK

"Stand on Zakarian's right." Samual motioned guiding her toward the entrance. A crisp breeze moved through the open palace doors, keeping her curls behind her shoulders, allowing the elaborate design of her gown to show. As she stepped out into the sun, it warmed her cheeks slightly, but the chill in the air made her grateful she was given the fur wrap. As she stepped up to Zakarian he held out his elbow implying that she should take it as they awaited their guests.

"Banphrionsa Alveen,. It seems your wear our kingdoms colors well." Banri Vailion approached from the bottom of the ramp. Her dark hair tied up in its usual formal style, a golden crown pinned into it raised high with its dark rubies matching her lips embellishing it in a simple design. Her gown was entirely burgundy velvet, her sleeves hung loose with fur at every edge, and she wore a solid fur cape, her clasp matching the ones her and Zakarian wore, only her cloak drug upon the ground behind her.

Standing in a line facing the oncoming carriages, she looked up and noticed Zakarian's crown looked much like hers in design, no rubies, though their outfits more than offset that. She nudged him softly and he looked down to her. "How do I address them? I haven't gotten to that lesson yet." She spoke in a frantic whisper. His lips curved in a grin as he squeezed her hand.

"Just address them as Queen, King, Prince or Princess, there is no going wrong there. As we said earlier, since they are here, they will have to abide by our customs. Which are really not that different from their own." She took a deep breath trying to mentally prepare for what was to come.

The first carriage was a pearl ivory color, ornamental carving embellished every inch. As it rolled to a stop at the bottom of the ramp, multiple guards rushed to open the doors and help the newly arrived royals. Alveen stood with a polite smile on her face as the first carriage emptied and three ladies met them at the top of the ramp.

"Queen Lovisa of Ireiell. It's been too long my friend." Banri wrapped the newcomer in a warm hug, which was returned. The Queen wore a long sleeve pale blue gown that swept the ground, it was plain other than a hood with white fur along her back. Her crown was a low sitting silver and aquamarine piece. She was a beautiful woman with perfect spiral curls hanging all the way to her knees. She should have prepared herself for perfection knowing all the monarchs are pure elven. At The Queens side were two young girls, each looked to be about five years old Alveen thought, which was actually much more in elven years she remembered. Even the young girls had the striking features of being elves. "Princess Ava and Brielle. You get more beautiful every time I see you." The girl curtsied to The Queen. "I am pleased to announce the return of Prince Zakarian and Princess Alveen." Zakarian bowed politely to all of them. Alveen curtsied, remembering to keep eye contact as she had been taught, to follow suit, which seemed to be the right answer as they copied as well.

"Prince Zakarian it's been so long. Ireiell has missed your visits."

"And I have missed it, hopefully soon we will be able to travel again and enjoy your beautiful shorelines." She continued walking and stopped in front of me studying me.

"My, time was rushed where ever you were placed. You have grown so much in such a short amount of time. It is a pleasure to see you again Princess, though I'm sure you don't remember. The girls however I do not believe you have met."

"Unfortunately, I cannot say that I remember many people at all. It is so lovely to meet you again, and it is a privilege to meet you both as well. We are all Princesses, perhaps we should spend time together?" The young girls grinned wide and curtsied.

"I'm sure they would enjoy that very much as the only other Princess is a little more…" She trailed off unable to find the appropriate word. "Well, you will meet her soon enough." She smiled patting Alveen's arm and continued on.

"Caspian will show you to your chambers, while we greet the others. We will join you in the dining hall." The Banri stated guiding them toward the white centaur waiting inside the entrance. Alveen admired them as they walked away.

"So where is Ireiell from here?" She asked Zakarian before the next carriage arrived.

"It is across the sea from here, only about a day of travel each way. They are almost entirely a peninsula, so majority of their land is islands and shoreline. Their main resource is salt, and fruits given the tropical climate, though they too see climate change."

Alveen tried to take in all the details that she could but was startled by the neighing of alicorns. There were no carriages this time, just a large entourage on the backs of the beautiful beasts, though it was still plain to see the royals in the group. The Banri smiled and began down the ramp, pausing midway to meet them. The girl sat atop her tan hued alicorn, very proud. Her short brown hair hung at her shoulders, resting on what looked like a leather corset over a dark green chiffon gown. The sleeves were long, and the skirt stopped about knee length. She wore brown leather pants and tall boots that were easily seen through the slits in her gown, much like one she had recently wore herself. Atop her head was a silver crown, with one large emerald in the center. She didn't smile, and she had a rugged demeanor about her. The other royal was an older man who was quick to dismount, greeting The Queen immediately.

"Ah King Hunter! How was the journey from Foresi?" The Banri held out her hand to The King. He was a short lean man from what she could tell. He wore a brown uniform accented with golden cords and a dark green velvet cape that was ground length. His hair may have been a dark brown at one point, but it was clearly graying. Salt and pepper hues shown through in his beard that hung below his chest. For as old as Alveen presumed he would have to be, he still looked physically fit.

"Only a few mountains to cross, not much trouble at all Queen Vailion." He took her hand and kissed it gently, standing straight as he walked with her up the ramp. "Prince Zakarian! Welcome home! Our hunts have missed you!" They clasped hands and pulled each other in for an embrace that was that of close friends.

"You will be pleased to know I have not lost my touch, we have already gone on multiple hunts since my return. Princess Alveen even proved herself." He gestured towards Alveen, who curtsied, keeping eye contact with him.

"Princess, you are more beautiful than I have heard." He bowed. "Is it true you are gifted with archery skills?"

"I wouldn't say gifted, but I believe I can hold my own." He laughed.

"Modesty from a royal, not something you see very often. Hold onto that Princess." He turned around and motioned the girl forward. "This is my daughter Princess Willow. She is quite gifted when it comes to hunting almost anything. I know you do not remember, but you use to be close." Alveen looked her in the eyes, not recognizing the dark brown they reflected.

"Pleasure to meet you again Princess Willow, I hope we will have a chance to become close again." She curtsied and smiled weakly.

"As do I, Princess Alveen." She wasn't very talkative but Alveen recognized the hurt in her voice, the same as Samual, that they were not recognized by someone close to them. The Banri repeated her instructions as Caspian returned. Alveen nudged Zakarian again, awaiting knowledge.

"King Hunter lost his wife during a battle with the Dorcha tribes, they are fierce hunters and warriors, Willow is the only heir to the throne. They trade in pelts and are excellent woodworkers." She nodded taking it in. "We must go to the bay to greet our next guests."

Alveen held onto Zakarian's arm, still unsure of how she was doing. Just because the first two kingdoms seemed to like them doesn't mean everyone was as kind. The Banri led the way, guards surrounding her. Alveen and Zakarian's guards fell in line around them as well. Out of the corner of her eye she could see Samual at her side, but she didn't allow herself to look and get distracted.

As they approached the pebbled shoreline they patiently stood and waited for whoever it was they were waiting for to reach them. Alveen wondered why they were even down here right now. They didn't wait nearly as long as they expected because only moments later a ship burst forth from the depths of the bay anchoring down and lowering a much more elaborate staircase than any pirate ship she was used to would have. Down the ship staircase came guards and two royal men. Zakarian leaned over to his younger sister, introducing them as they made their way to the proud royals waiting to welcome them to the kingdom.

"This is King Bowen, with the long black hair, and Prince Viktor, with the short well-groomed hair, of Krumvite. Their kingdom is unique in the sense that it is entirely underwater. You could compare it to Atlantis from what you know." Her eyes widened, an underwater civilization? The knowledge and possibilities continued to grow.

"Is that Princess Alveen I see? My, my you are beautiful site." The Prince approached her after greeting The Banri.

"Do I know him?" She whispered quickly to Zakarian.

"Yes, you had a very close friendship with him."

"Oh, my apologies, Princess. My excitement overcame me. Prince Viktor. You were once a dear friend of mine." He bowed taking her hand, kissing the top.

"It's a privilege to meet you, again, Prince Viktor. I seem to be learning that I was close with a few others as well. I apologize that I am unable to remember, hopefully we will have time to get to know each other, again." The Prince brought his hands together behind his back smiling nervously at her. He was cute in a boyish way, though as it seemed almost all male elves were taller than her. He had a lean build, though his shoulders couldn't have been much wider than her own.

"I would wish for nothing more." She stared at him, his black hair shining in the sun and his eyes a deep blue like the sea. She was caught up for a moment until King Bowen walked towards them.

"Ah I see Prince Viktor has managed to charm his way back to The Princess." The King smiled and bowed to her and Zakarian. "It is so wonderful to see you both home safely."

"It's wonderful to be home, King Bowen. I feel as though you may see The Princess more in the future. She was infatuated with a legend where we previously were that resembles much of what your kingdom is. I'm sure when the time is right, she would love to visit." Alveen glanced at Zakarian. Was that appropriate to invite yourself to someone's kingdom?

"Seaweed and trenches! Is that so Princess?"

"From what I understand yes, an underwater civilization sounds fascinating to me."

"Once it is safe for you to travel, you will finally be able to see our home Princess. I'm sure Prince Viktor wouldn't object." Prince Viktor blushed, scowling at his father. "We must go prepare for brunch in our chambers, but we will see you soon Prince Zakarian and Princess Alveen." We all bowed and parted ways.

Over the mountains a small jet approached. After reaching the shoreline it hovered above the pebble beach. This jet was plain white with no markings or designs on it, but it shined in the sun like it was freshly cleaned. Alveen hadn't even seen the door that was now opening allowing a carpeted staircase to descend. Almost double the amount of guards, a man and woman stepped off the private jet, stern looks plastered to their pristine faces, clothing like they just came out of an imperative meeting.

"This is Queen Karolyn and King Ronan of Loxley, they are twins ruling side by side." Zakarian explained as we walked towards them. They looked like twins for certain. He had short cut blonde hair, and she had a blonde short bob haircut, their eyes both a similar green to The Queens. Alveen curtsied, keeping eye contact as she approached.

"Princess. Quite a surprise to see you. I trust you are adjusting well to being home?" King Ronan stated in a monotone voice.

"Quite well, thank-you. How was your journey?" She asked trying to stay polite, they did not seem as friendly as the others.

"It went rather quickly. And obviously, we had no issues." Queen Karolyn chimed in with an 'isn't it obvious' tone. Alveen simply nodded. "Prince Zakarian, I expect you will be looking for a partner soon? Better sooner than later." She stated bluntly. Alveen hadn't even thought about Zakarian being with someone since everyone had been putting the pressure on her. But he was much older and would take the throne long before her. The twins walked off towards the palace.

"They were charming." Zakarian said to Banri Vailion.

"They may be strange but they are a strong ally to have, and they are simply honest in a brute way." She began walking, "Let us head back to the palace."

Alveen's heels clicked on the stone floor as they entered the palace. "I need to go freshen up. We will be meeting everyone in the dining hall within the hour." The Queen walked away towards her wing of the palace.

"I will meet you there." Zakarian said walking back towards his wing of the palace. The guards had dispersed since everyone was in the palace again. Alveen stood alone in the corridor unsure where to go. The entrance to the palace did have a sitting area off to the side that she had yet to enjoy.

Standing tall she walked passed multiple pillars wrapped in vines, noticing they were slowly turning from green to brown. Mysti did say the season change was today, Alveen wondered how quick the season change would be here.

• • •

The glass doors opened into a small but extravagant room that sat on the bottom floor of the turret hosting a large stone fireplace against the far wall. The room had a few windows that reached all the way to the floor and stretched far above. Wall scones decorated the stone walls, and multiple chairs and sofas sat sporadically throughout the area. She enjoyed this time to herself, to revel in the magic and the new life she was now living. She knelt down in front of the fireplace, enjoying the warmth on her shoulders and cheeks. Standing up she went to the corner of the room, running her fingers across the familiar fabric that adorned her bodice and sat down, finally letting out a breath that she could relax now that she had met everyone. She heard footsteps outside the room, choosing to ignore them because she was by the entry and no one ever comes in this room.

Or so she thought. Two gentlemen rushed into the room, the one behind short and plump, calling after the man in front of him. "Your Majesty, we must properly announce you." The man stood in front of the fire warming his bare hands. He was towering over the other wearing a full fur cape. He whipped his head around, still he hadn't seen her in the corner as he was facing away from her.

"I do not need pleasantries. I have arrived, let Her Majesty know, but I do not need a charade of guards and introductions. I wish to have a few moments to myself before I play must play political niceness." His voice was calm, but raspy and deep. It drew Alveen in hearing him speak. The small man rushed out of the room closing the doors behind him. Now she was stuck in the room alone with this man. He took off his cape, tossing it on a nearby chair revealing a solid gold crown, no design or embellishment, just a golden ring with peaks and valleys that sat on his dark brown hair that was cut extremely short at the sides blended to meet the longer hair styled at the top. His hair extended down his face trimmed perfectly to match his sharp masculine jaw covered in a thick beard. His neck showed large muscles she would have guessed rippled down his back. She crossed one leg over the other quietly and watched him for a moment. He was in a tucked black button up, standing tall. She couldn't help but notice that his shoulders were massively broad, and his physique seemed like he endured hard labor often, which she could only tell because he wore fitted clothes.

He slowly turned around letting out a breath. He turned as his eyes met hers. He knew she was there the whole time. Standing up folding her arms over her chest with authority, she let out a smile. "I wanted to give you a moment before interrupting, but I suppose I should leave you to yourself." He was obviously royal, but she had not met him yet. He stood tall, imitating her arm fold, looking her up and down like he wasn't sure if he was going to say something rude or not anything at all. There was a long silence as if he was going to say nothing. She raised her brow to him as she slowly walked towards the door.

"Who are you? I don't think we've ever met." He stepped closer to her. She could clearly see his face now. His strong jaw sat tense at the moment, but she could see it clearly, even through the thick beard groomed perfectly on his face and eyes like none she had ever seen before. Colors like swirling molten gold, the lightest brown caressed by the reflection of the warm light the scones provided. She averted her eyes, pretending to focus on the pattern of fabric on the chair she stood behind.

"I believe it is you who should be introducing yourself to me. But" she paused, returning to meet his eyes, this stranger made her feel unrecognizably confident. "I would hate for you to have to start early playing political niceness. Is that what you called it?" She smirked at him, not able to break their eye contact. Something about this man made her not want to leave the room. She did not feel intimidated by him, though he was more than a head taller than her and could probably lift her with one arm. He smirked back, one side of his mouth curving up. His face was young but defined and worn. She guessed he was not much older than Zakarian maybe.

He said nothing but walked around and leaned against the back of the sofa in front of where she was now standing. "Princess Alveen." His throat rumbled as he spoke her name. His smile dropped but he still looked interested. Alveen curtsied, keeping eye contact with the stranger.

"I'm afraid I have to admit I don't recognize you. I seem to have forgotten quite a bit." She joked not knowing how much this man knew about her.

"I was unaware you had returned. I expect your brother is back as well?"

"Yes, returned just recently. Still learning the customs as I'm sure you can tell." She could smell cinnamon and burning firewood. She took a deep breath in, pretending not to be intoxicated by the comfort it brought her. She wanted to compliment him on his scent, but even she knew that was inappropriate.

"Hardly." He eyed her, unable to get over her stance and how she carried herself so confidently in the midst of a stranger, let alone him being that stranger. Most people were often intimidated. He admired her gown, noticing her sheer shoulders, all the while she was doing the same to him, noticing the fit of his shirt around his arms, and a chest that looked like he'd been a blacksmith his whole life. "Hardly what I would expect of The Princess from Cosaint." He continued, masking any tone of interest he had before, sounding as if he meant to insult her. Other women he had encountered were so unlike the woman that stood before him now. Her self-respect glowed from her expressions, and her dignity was still intact, even after they spoke. Most were after him for his crown and fortune, and he had never given them the time of day.

"Well, as lovely as this conversation has been, I'm sure I'll see you soon?" She began walking out the door, making sure she added a hint of sarcasm to her comment. He seemed to have a slight arrogance about him. The last thing she wanted to do was help it get worse. He admired her curves as she walked away. "Are you joining the rest of us for brunch?" She threw over her shoulder as if she had forgotten to ask.

"Doubtful."

"Why are you here if not for the royal walk and the festivities?" she spoke forcefully, curious as to who this royal stranger was, but trying to be careful not to insult him. He stood and walked closer to her. She tried standing proud, though she only stood to this man's chest. He was mysterious, and it bothered her that he wouldn't make known his identity to her.

"Wouldn't you like to know, Princess." He teased leaning down towards her ear, making her face heat up.

"Ah! King Luka! It is a privilege to be escorting you today. Your chambers are ready now. We are so sorry for the delay." Caspian stood at the door, taking notice of Alveen's cheeks.

"Princess, are you alright?"

"Perfectly fine, Caspian. Thank-you. The fire warmed this room quickly." She spoke to him with her hands together in front of her. She turned back towards her guest, "King Luka." she said as both a statement and question. "I expect I'll be seeing you around." She turned toward Caspian, placing her fist respectfully over her heart, nodding to him. He gave an approving smile and returned the gesture. She strode away towards the dining hall, not looking back over her shoulder to see him again because she could feel his gaze on her back.

~CHAPTER XV~
THE NIGHT SKY BALL

Alveen entered the dining hall where only a few of the guests were waiting. The Royals of Foresi, Ireiell and Krumvite were either in their seats or in front of the oversized fireplace that sat behind the head of the table. Rays of sunlight shined down from the ceiling. The branches above parted just enough to fully illuminate the room. Samual and a few of her other guards were present as well.

"Pleasure to see you Princess" Samual said as he was approaching her. She smiled as she turned to converse with him.

"Where were you? I thought you were to be my personal guard?" She joked.

"Strict orders by The Prince to give you space as well. Why? Did something happen?" He questioned with concern.

"Nothing I couldn't handle myself." He stepped to the side as The Royals of Loxley entered the room. Alveen approached Princess Willow and King Hunter by the fireplace as the staff filled the table with different delicacies.

"Princess, I was hoping I would get a chance to speak with you again." Alveen said and she approached Princess Willow. She turned around, her face remained unreadable for only a moment before a small smile broke across.

"I have missed you Princess Alveen." She stood giving her a nervous hug. "I'm sorry, I know you don't remember, but you were one of my best friends." Alveen smiled.

"Please don't apologize. I have a feeling we can still be the close friends we were. I actually wanted to invite you to possibly train with me tomorrow, maybe even teach me a bit since I am essentially starting over? I'm not sure how long you will be here for." Princess Willow glowed.

"Yes! I would love to! Oh Alveen, I cannot wait."

"Do you mind if I join?" King Hunter stepped in.

"Not at all, Your Majesty, I look forward to gaining back close friends."

"I taught Willow all she knows, maybe I'll have some pointers to help you learn faster." He smiled and chuckled as he turned to face the fire again.

"He taught me much of what I know as well." Her brother's voice made her relax a little as he joined in. "Maybe I can join too."

"Sounds perfect." Alveen thought back to King Luka, she didn't even know another royal was coming. Maybe she would ask more about him and his kingdom later, now was a time to re-build her friendships. Prince Viktor and King Bowen joined the group shortly after.

The door flung open and The Banri glided in gracefully making her way to her spot at the head of the table. "Please take a seat everyone. I'm sure you're all hungry from your journey." We all sat. Zakarian on one side, Princess Willow on her other, and across from them were King Bowen and Prince Viktor. She glanced around and saw King Luka was absent. The Princess was not going to bring it up given he made it obvious he would not be there.

Princess Willow spent most of brunch picking fun at Prince Viktor while his father, King Bowen, would cheer her on. Alveen felt relaxed around them, as if they had been friends for much longer than she remembered.

After enjoying an eventless, yet memorable lunch, all the royals were able to take a small break before the walk would begin. Alveen had started to gather that Prince Viktor was a fan of literature, she thought it a wise way to spend time by inviting him and Princess Willow to the library.

"I've never been inside the library here. I expect it's much more extravagant than ours." Viktor said. She led them down the hall, all her guards in tow. "You have serious security, don't you princess?"

"Are you really saying that after what just happened Prince Viktor?" Willow commented. "It would be the same if anything happened to any of us. She's just lucky she survived."

The next few hours were spent touring the palace, aside from her chamber that was still under reconstruction. They met with all the royals at the entrance, preparing for the walk.

"Princess Alveen, join me please." The Banri called to her. She left Willow and Viktor with their fathers as she stepped towards her grandmother, brother and King Luka standing beside them. Her chest tightened for a moment as they held eye contact. He let the slightest smirk show but pushed it aside, leaving a stoic mask as he stood silently beside The Queen.

"Yes, Your Majesty?" She said as she approached, trying to ignore the tension in the air, though she was probably the only one feeling it.

"I would like you to meet King Luka. We were unsure if he would make it, but we are so happy that he was able to join us for this important day and to celebrate your return. He is the King of the northern most kingdom, Bulgrakta." He gave a deep, respectful bow, holding eye contact with her, giving her that hint of a smile.

"It's a pleasure to meet you, Your Highness." His voice was professional and now she understood what he meant in their earlier conversation, though she did wish to see more of his casual side that he seemed to let show earlier. She curtsied in response.

"Likewise, Your Majesty." She tried to sound uninterested. He gave her a subtle raise of his brow. She saw his attire was much more regal than she had previously seen him. A black uniform with golden cords, black dress boots and he even had a near matching cape like Zakarians from earlier, however his was a few shades darker, closer matching his ensemble.

"I was speaking to The Queen about you, shortly before you arrived." His husky, deep voice made her heart feel light as he spoke to her, though now she was worried she may have acted inappropriately toward him earlier.

"Is that so? I do hope it was all pleasant." She commented, keeping a neutral expression.

"King Luka had a marvelous idea, my dear. The ball tonight requires an escort. King Luka is interested in getting to know you further and will be taking you tonight." Alveen wasn't sure what to say. Her and Samual were official, weren't they? What was she supposed to do, insult an ally king?

"Oh, that's a very generous offer. Though I don't think that will be necessary." The Queen laughed at The Princess's response.

"No, my dear, you must attend with a non-relative royal member. Zakarian already has a couple beautiful ladies to take." She glanced at him now kneeling down while talking to Princess Ava and Brielle. "I will be attending with King Hunter, Queen Lovisa with King Ronan, Queen Karolyn with King Bowen, and

Princess Willow with Prince Viktor. You with King Luka." She wanted to argue. She didn't want to hurt Samual.

"Of course, Grandmother." Zakarian stood back up.

"However, the walk you are able to be with me, King Luka and grandmother are paired up for this one since they are both unpaired right now." He held out his arm. King Luka already turned away. Alveen nudged him.

"What am I supposed to do!?" Her voice frantic. "Samual will be so hurt. I have no interest in this man." Zakarian sighed.

"Samual is simply courting you, all that means is that he has been granted approval to *try* and win your affections, however, the door has been opened for other suitors to do the same." He looked her in the eyes, addressing her confusion. "Thank-you, by the way, for avoiding that conversation with me. I nearly didn't believe him." He jokingly scolded her. She pinched her face apologetically. "Samual is aware you will have others trying to win your hand. He is strong hearted and prepared for that. Do not push off other options yet, especially King Luka, you are not official with anyone until you are engaged." Alveen relaxed not realizing how courting and suitors actually worked.

"How much do you know about him?"

"He is the last of his line. Mother drown on a ship accident and father was recently lost in one of the battles. He was hidden in a village, out of knowledge until the past few years. This is the first time I've met him. I heard he worked for a blacksmith. He is from Bulgrakta, which is known for harsh cold, but they are also known for mining and blacksmith products.

Very strong, tough people in his tribe." She smiled thinking of her thoughts about him earlier and how some of them weren't very far off from the truth. "And let me be frank with you, grandmother *will* push for your relationship with him, simply because he is elven, in need of an heir and they have been a steady, trustworthy ally. It would be a great political match." Alveen tensed at the mention of an heir, something she was no longer able to give. She ignored the secret that welled inside her. She would choose Samual anyways.

"Honestly? How old is he though? Shouldn't I be with someone closer to my age." All of this new information was spinning in her head as they descended the ramp, heading into the crowd that was split like they were expecting a parade.

"He's actually only slightly younger than I am." Zakarian looked down to her, seeing that she was taking all of this in. "Just give this all a chance. You have the right to deny anyone that tries to court you, and ultimately it is up to you." She looked to see Samual walking alongside the precession a few rows behind them. Alveen nodded in agreement.

"Princess! Princess!" A young girl called out from the crowd. Alveen waved and masked her concern and confusion with a proper and professional smile. "You are so strong!" The young girl was running alongside them behind a row of adults. Luka glanced back at her, making eye contact.

The walk consisted of going through some of the local businesses. They stopped in multiple shops Alveen had never been in, meeting the business owners. Alveen gripped Zakarian's arm with excitement as they approached Fennryr's Bakery. She glanced back to Samual making sure he noticed.

"Samual!" She called, he joined at her side. She let go of Zakarian's arm and wrapped her hands around Samual's, breaking from the walk to go ahead to the Bakery. Behind her a few of the royals were puzzled. "Fennryr!" she called politely as she entered.

"Ah! Banphrionsa Alveen! I would say this is a surprise, but I have been preparing for you!" he spoke quietly but eager. He walked around the counter as a few of the other royals walked in, including King Luka. "Here! For you, my beautiful Banphrionsa. Made fresh as usual, per your request." He handed her a small plate and fork with the familiar dessert that she requested any time she went into his shop.

"You are so kind Fennryr! I can't believe you did this for me." She leaned in to hug the baker and he placed a respectful peck on her cheek.

"Anything for you Banphrionsa! Business has been much busier since you last visited."

"What and none for me?" Samual joked. The baker chuckled and reached behind the counter.

"Ah, but you prefer something different Sir Samual." He handed him a steaming muffin, filling the air with a lemony scent, though Alveen was still nibbling at her perfected dessert.

"You truly are the best, old friend." The two began to walk out standing next to Banri Vailion and King Luka, who were patiently waiting for them.

"I didn't realize you knew so many of the villagers already Princess." The Banri said with a smile, appreciative that her granddaughter was so comfortable among her own tribe. Her eagerness would help calm the citizens, which was the whole purpose of this walk after all.

"Samual has helped by guiding me around and introducing me to some wonderful, loyal people." She squeezed his arm in appreciation. He looked at her and gave a small bow. Luka had diverted his attention elsewhere, not paying attention to them at all.

"Oh Princess, Masgo has informed me your order is ready." She smiled in response.

Once back in formation they continued to the clearing for the afternoon tea with nobles. Alveen had yet to meet any of the Barons, Viscounts or Lords yet. Alveen started towards her chair near the head of the table. King Luka stood still behind her chair, pulled out for her with an unreadable expression. She slowed seeing this, raising an eyebrow. He gestured for her to sit but said nothing.

"Thank-you King Luka." She sat letting him assist pushing her chair in, and he sat next to her now separating her from Zakarian. He was too occupied with the young Princesses telling jokes to notice. She did not make eye contact with the King, just simply placed her hands folded on her lap focusing on the soft feel of the satin skirt.

The nobles sat at the table, speaking quietly with some of the royals. "King Luka, how is Bulgrakta these days?" He didn't make eye contact with the noble speaking.

"Frozen as usual, but my people are hearty, hardworking and strong. They keep us running better than ever." He stated simply sitting back enjoying a hot cup of tea. The noble nodded and began conversation with Queen Lovisa, talking about their beautiful coasts and of visits soon.

"Grandmother, if I may, I do have one last place I wish to visit. May I be excused early to prepare for the ball this evening?"

"Of course, dear."

"Allow me to accompany you. I wouldn't mind retiring early as well." King Luka stood holding out his oversized, vein embossed forearm. She accepted his arm standing, addressing the rest of the table.

"It was quite the enjoyable afternoon, I hope to see you all this evening." She bowed her head to the table, holding the crock of Luka's arm. She whispered to him, still holding a smile on her face and they passed the rest of the Royals who paid them no attention at this point. "Is this necessary, King Luka? I do have half a dozen guards who follow me around."

"I am more interested in seeing who else you visit on a regular basis." He was looking forward, keeping pace with her.

"What is that supposed to mean?" She was genuinely confused by his remark.

"I've never seen a royal as comfortable as you are among their citizens, that's all" He looked down to her, her eyes on the road ahead of her avoiding eye contact. "You treat them as equals, not inferiors." He didn't sound disgusted but impressed but the fact.

She thought for a moment about how to reply. "I guess being away, I don't have experience acting as a royal would. I've always looked at a person's character base on how they treat their inferiors. I am no better than any of them." Their conversation was low. Guards fell in around them, both his and hers, keeping their distance to give them privacy. Samual was a constant presence in her mind, though King Luka had not expressed romantic interest as Zakarian suggested, all she could think was how uncomfortable Samual must be. There was nothing wrong with being a friend to an ally king.

"You are unique Princess." A friendly smile appeared within his groomed beard, causing a surprised look by The Princess as he made eye contact with her.

"So I have been told." She looked to him "Not what you expected?" he didn't answer right away, she assumed he would not answer again since that seemed to be a tendency of his.

"Far from it." He finally whispered leaning to her. They arrived at her destination, the butcher, where her kill awaited. He gave a confused look but said nothing.

"I have a few things that need to be arranged here, that's all. You can wait outside if you wish." He guided her inside ignoring her suggestion.

"Much more regal than our last encounter, Banphrionsa." Masgo acknowledged her outfit as he reached out, bowing, as he held her hand. "I see Samual relayed my message." He nodded to Samual standing to the side.

"As you can see she is excited. She couldn't leave the tea with nobles quick enough." He chuckled. "Masgo, may I introduce King Luka of Bulgrakta." Masgo bowed.

"Your Majesty, pleased to meet you." He nodded respectfully to the butcher in response.

"I hear you and The Princess are familiar." He directed towards Masgo.

"Yes, she keeps me busy." He chuckled walking to the back. "I will return in a moment."

"The Princess is quite the shot. Showed up most of our nobles and guards at the last hunt we organized." King Luka raised an eyebrow looking down at her. His eyes glowing as he learned more about her.

"Is that so?" She rolled her eyes at his question, not replying to it.

"Here we go Princess! Just as requested. Now, the meat has been dispersed as directed, nothing wasted." She leaned forward looking through the box on the counter ahead of her, filled with fur blankets and accessories such as hair combs, rings, necklace pendants and even a crown made from the bleached bones of the animal. Luka leaned forward surprised at the contents. She reached in and picked up the tiara, small bones protruded up the front of the crown, and diamonds sparkled sitting into the unusual creation. She loved it, it would fit perfectly into her collection and the gems disguised the true material.

"This is magnificent. Your craftsmanship is among the finest." She praised.

"Banphrionsa, you are too kind. I know you did not order those, but I couldn't help myself. You have more than filled the stomachs of my family." He paused, grateful. "Would you like me to get this delivered to your chamber?" Masgo questioned.

"That won't be necessary. I can help The Princess." Luka interjected.

"Are you sure? I don't doubt your strength…" Alveen started giving his arms and torso a once over. "But it's really no issue to have others take care of this." He ignored the suggestion again, throwing the set of antlers masgo brought out over his shoulders and carrying the large box in his grip. He gave her a raised eyebrow curving one side of his mouth.

"I may be a King, but I do remember how to be chivalrous."

"I can carry my own things. Thank-you King Luka." She extended her arms out, anticipating the weight of the box that didn't come.

"Lead the way Princess." She walked out thanking Masgo again for his incredible work, ensuring that she would return. Walking down the street towards the palace, guards dispersed. Luka looked happy for a second as she glanced at him carrying her items.

"I can help King Luka. Please, let me carry something." He ignored her request, not bothering to respond. "This silent treatment is …..." He glanced at her, but she didn't even know how to finish without insulting him. He still didn't respond.

As they entered the palace Samual walked to the front of them, approaching her. "Princess Alveen, your chambers are finished if you wish to take your items there."

"Perfect! Thank-you Samual." She touched his arm. They all walked towards her door. It looked exactly the same as before. She pushed open the door hesitantly to an unfamiliar room. It looked nothing like it did before minus the balcony which was still intact. The floor was replaced with stone that matched the ceiling height surround of the fireplace. It looked like a large slab of stone carved intricately to replicate the design of the ornamental fireplace in the entry hall. A large branch chandelier hung with crystals in front of the balcony reflecting the sunlight. Wind blew against the golden curtains that now hung on the newly replaced glass doors. In the center of the room towered an old-world canopy bed frame, driftwood and branches made up the shape of this much like the other she had, though this one had golden flecking throughout the knots and grain and burgundy curtains draped over the frame. Luka stepped in behind her observing just as much as she was.

"This is nice Princess." He walked quietly around the room, setting everything down at the foot of the bed. "Where do you want the antlers?" he twisted his wrist floating them in midair until receiving instruction. She stood there folding her arms observing him and then slowly pointed above the engraved mantel. Breaking eye contact, he moved it where she requested, making sure it attached to the stone securely. Her guards stood outside the door that was still open. Bending down she pulled out a lush fur blanket made from the hide as requested. The fur had been conditioned in a delicate way, the back covered in silk. "You have good taste." The king acknowledged as she sprawled the first blanket over the end of her bed, and placed a smaller second blanket, that was in the bottom of the box, over one of the chairs that sat in front of the fireplace. She looked around the room, taking in the new décor.

• • •

"Are you okay Princess?" Luka asked, only barley brushing his hand against her fingers, startling her.

"Perfectly fine. It's recently remodeled, just appreciating the upgrade, that's all." She pulled her arm away from his hand. "So, I will see you tonight?"

"I look forward to it. I feel I have much to learn about you Princess. I will meet you by the entrance." He grabbed her hand bowing but did not place a kiss on it. They locked eyes, both masking uncertain feelings.

Luka was interested in The Princess because she was confident, and she didn't mind putting him in his place. She seemed to be the only one that didn't think him rude when he was silent but understood it as his form of communication. He spoke to her more today than he spoke to many of the other royals his entire life.

Samual passed the King as he left the room bowing to him before he approached Alveen. She stood there, worried. "Alveen." He stated standing in front of her.

"Samual. I am so sorry, I had no idea Royals were even coming, let alone that any of them would take interest in me." Her hands were folded in front of her as she explained. He reached out and held her upper arms, looking her in the eyes, running his thumbs through the fur wrapped around her.

"Alveen." He smiled. "Don't worry. I knew what I was getting into when I asked to court you. Now, The King doesn't need to ask permission, though we aren't positive what his intentions are yet. . . . But" he stopped.

"It's my decision. I know. Can I be honest with you?" She asked looking to him. He nodded with concern. "I'm not comfortable with this. It feels unfaithful and I am not okay with it. I hope you will understand, but aside from a kiss on the cheek, until decisions are final, I am not okay with more than that." They had shared a kiss before, and she refused to share moments like that with more than one man at a time.

"I can respect that." He nodded relieved. "However, I must not let this interfere with my position as well. So." He sighed, "I will be waiting outside your chamber to escort you to the entrance where King Luka will be waiting for you. But I will still be near all night. Perhaps I will still get time with you."

"Samual, you are amazing." She rested a hand on his cheek, feeling his cheek tense with a sad smile before he turned and walked out, closing the doors behind him. Mysti entered shortly after.

"Are you ready to woo all of your suitors?" she excitedly proclaimed clapping quietly as she approached the newly remodeled closet.

"All of my suitors?" she scoffed. "So far I seem to only have one. Though there have been other suggestions." Mysti turned around popping out of the closet,

"Rumor has it King Luka has been eyeing you."

"King Luka and I are establishing a friendship." Mysti's eyes filled with disbelief. "It is possible to just be friends." Alveen confirmed with certainty in her voice.

● ● ●

"We will see. In the meantime, I believe you have a very important ball to prepare for. And it looks like there is a newly remodeled closet and vanity waiting to be used." Alveen entered her newly acquired closet, with its own vanity at the very back. One side overfilled with fine gowns, many of which looked similar to her pervious now destroyed ones. She reached out to see her seafoam goddess gown and her teal custom-made gown from Samual had managed to survive. The other side organized strategically with pants, skirts, tops and a jewelry case displaying all the crowns and matching sets of jewelry, and accessories like jackets, hats and scarves. Across the top of both sides were dozens of shoes of all styles and colors. "I suggest matching your date, as a sign of encouragement." Mysti suggested with a smile and a wink.

Samual stood in the hallway outside Alveen's chambers waiting for her to emerge for the ball that was to follow the royal walk. Zakarian was already by the entrance with his guards and multiple royals, including the two Princesses. Samual decided to go clean shaven to show off his fierce features and his hair groomed to perfection. He stood tall in a fully black suit with a burgundy button up, both fitting nicely to his toned figure, and a black silk tie resting on his chest. Pacing, his footsteps echoed through the hallway until he heard another's approaching.

"Why Sir Samual, it seems you may be anxious with the way you're burning footsteps into this stone." His heart fluttered momentarily at the sound of her voice. Lifting his gaze, he followed the dark, flared organza as it cinched mid-thigh transforming to the black silk that hugged The Princess's form perfectly until revealing her bare shoulders. He took in the simple elegance of the gown and glittering jewelry, until finally he rested on her mesmerizing face. She had a darker lipstick than he'd ever seen her wear, matching the burgundy gown she wore earlier. Dark eye makeup accented by golden sparkle that enhanced the brilliance of her eyes and cheeks. Her hair was twisted into an elegant array that was tied back trailing over her right shoulder ending at the bottom of her ribcage. Resting on top of her curls sat the same golden tiara that stood a hand tall above her head all day. "You clean up quite well." Her voice flirtatious. She stood taller than usual in her pumps of black silk with the heel wrapped in golden metal vines and leaves, but Samual still had a couple inches on her. "I do prefer you in suits after all, the one you wore when we met was particularly flattering."

"I didn't realize you noticed." He grinned seductively.

"I didn't at first, until we were on the plane." She paused, slowly emphasizing every step she took toward him, making her hips sway just enough to grab his attention. "When I realized we had a real past, and I was willing to take a chance on the handsome stranger." They were still standing over an arm's length apart grinning at each other. He cleared his throat.

"Well, I thought I cleaned up nicely as well, but then here you are outshining me yet again Your Highness." He smiled looking to the ground as he walked towards her, holding her gaze for a moment as he spoke. She blushed innocently.

"Flattery will get you everywhere" she repeated the familiar words to him before taking his arm.

"In all seriousness, Princess, you look magnificent." She dropped her cocky facade for a moment when she heard his comment.

"Do you really think so? It's been quite a nerve racking day for me." She smoothed out the shining fabric over her stomach as she spoke "And I am impressed that I am able to walk in high heels still." She giggled enjoying this time alone with Samual. They approached the entrance; King Luka was not among the royals standing there. She turned around, seeing his figure standing outside the entry room where they had their first encounter. "Sir Samual, I apologize but I do believe I should join my date." She said professionally gesturing towards the side room. He nodded, releasing her hand with a glint of sadness in his dark eyes.

Taking in a deep breath, she slowly began towards the tall figure standing in the entry room, facing the fireplace. Her gown trailed behind her, glimmering in the glow of the flames on the wall as she approached. Black pants, a black silk button up shirt fitting him about as tightly as her gown fit her, revealing every muscle in his back and arms. His sleeves were folded nicely above his elbows and the shadows of the flames danced against his forearms. Walking towards him, she felt confident. How did this man not intimidate her? He seemed to intimidate even the Loxley twins. She wasn't sure what to say since their conversations had been minimal. She walked in, her shoes clicking softly on the stone below them. Instead of starting a conversation she decided to walk up and stand next to him, silently as he usually was. He stayed leaning against the back of the couch, facing the flames, but his attention landed on her. She could only think to describe him a well dress viking.

"Punctual, I can appreciate that." Still no smile.

"Did you expect me to be late?" She asked crossing one arm over her waist, holding onto her other that hung at her side.

He stood up straight facing her. "I could say the same about you, Your Majesty." Her jokingly prideful appearance returned.

"Did you expect me not to show up?" He playfully mocked her, keeping his face serious.

"The thought crossed my mind." She turned and sat on the back of the couch, still leaving room between them, looking up to him even more than she previously did. "But I am a little fun to be around, I expect you didn't want to miss out on that." She joked breaking an exaggerated smile across her face, twisting a curl that hung at her chest. She laughed at her own imitation of a spoiled Princess. He rolled his eyes but his face relaxed. He turned around and sat as she did, only he left very little room between them.

"Though that may be so, I am merely here because I feel you and I could develop a great friendship." He admitted, though with his close proximity to her, she wasn't sure she believed that. "I'm sure you've heard I didn't grow up being royal either, so you and I are much alike in that aspect." His admission made her curious.

"May I ask you something?" She eyed him confused. He looked at her expectantly, waiting. "Suggestions have been made, and I mean no offense by this but do you.... Are you planning on courting me? Is that why you are here?" He sat quiet for a moment before looking to her and giving a deep chuckle. The sound made her chest rumble, and she loved it.

"No." he stated bluntly. She waited. He noticed she was expecting more of an explanation, so he continued. "I truly am only interested in a friendship at the moment. I would not have traveled this far to court someone I didn't know or had never seen before." With his last comment his eyes fell over her gown and back up to her face. She was mildly relieved. They really did have similar mindsets. Perhaps it was from being thrown into all of this. "Besides, I see that your heart is elsewhere, and as strikingly unpleasant as I may seem to everyone else, loyalty is the most important thing to me." He crossed his arms looking at her. "And I have no desire to fight for a woman's affection, even if she is a Princess." Alveen was shocked. This gentleman beside her, this King, was so morally righteous and everything she had heard from others showed he was rude and impossible. "I think this is more than I have ever talked to another royal." He stated standing up, extending his elbow to her. She now saw he wore a black tie, blending into his outfit this evening, and he picked up a suit coat with silk wings. Alveen watched intently as he stretched his arms into the sleeves.

"Your secret is safe with me." She accepted his arm. "Your Majesty." He glued his somber expression to his face as they went to join the already in line precession. The Banri and King Hunter led the paired off royals across the village to the training grounds.

As they approached Alveen could see the romantic glow of thousands of lit candles, some which lingered above like low lying stars. Out of the corner of her eye she could see Luka admiring her. They had been silent during the entire walk across the village.

"Did you dress to match me this evening?" He asked suddenly. She looked to him.

"Of course not. Black and gold just looked ravishing on me." She winked jokingly.

● ● ●

"Nothing has ever been more true, Princess." He spoke in a low whisper. His flattering remark caused her to catch her breath. Did the impossible, rude, unbearable king of the frozen tundra just give her a compliment?

They stood near the staircase that led up to Leigheas's home where Alveen first woke up. The Banri walked up the stairs to address her kingdom from the railing above.

"My beautiful Cosaintians. I am grateful for the opportunity to celebrate with you all today. Not only do we celebrate strength in our kingdom through the recent attack directly aimed toward our Banphrionsa Alveen, we remain vigilant and we will not falter." The crowd cheered at her encouragement. "We also celebrate the alliances we have made and come to cherish. We celebrate to thank Queen Karolyn and King Ronan of Loxley, King Bowen and Prince Viktor of Krumvite, Queen Lovisa and Princesses Ava and Brielle of Ireiell, King Luka of Bulgrakta and King Hunter and Princess Willow of Foresi" The crowd cheered again in gratitude for the five kingdoms that had come to join them. "I don't wish to keep you from your festivities long, but I want to extend gratitude to every single individual that has helped this day come together, and everyone who has assisted in the repair of the palace. Please, enjoy the evening under the night sky! Without further ado, let us celebrate with the official change of season!"

With her last statement she clapped her hands together above her head and pushed them forward, a forceful breeze blowing around. Alveen looked around, observing as the sunset lit the trees aglow. The greenery around her faded to striking hues of reds, oranges, yellows, golds and browns, wrapped together like the dancing of flames. The glow from the candles brightened with the vibrant colors blazing as the sun faded from the sky.

Music began to play, and the clearing quickly filled with creatures swaying in the starlight, surrounded by the warm glow that emitted a dreamy ambiance. royals stepped onto the dance floor, swirling around, solidifying the bonds they had worked to keep.

"I am not the most graceful dancer." Alveen admitted to King Luka, who stared at all the twirling creatures.

"Unfortunately for you, I am." He led her to an open spot among the others. Wrapping his arm around her waist, holding her body close to his he extended their intertwined hands out, gently pushing her into a twirl, letting her fall back into his embrace. In her heels she stood only to his shoulders. She spent their dance taking in his features. His beard looked as if he may have trimmed it since it now sat only a mere inch or two off his skin., the fullness still didn't hide his masculine cheek bones and jaw line. He always wore a stoic expression that made guards and royals alike avoid him. She met his eyes, and he held her gaze, unable to look away as his face relaxed. She studied his eyes, around his pupil and the edge of his irises were a dark brown, but between was reflective of the romantic radiance that surrounded them. They reminded her of fall and a fireplace. His hair was cut short on the sides, drawing focus to the top that was grown out enough to be pushed to the side, but not enough that it was in his line of vision, styled neatly in the center of his solid gold crown. She took in a deep breath, making him break the gaze. Without a word, he lifted her effortlessly off the ground, spinning her in a circle as the other dancers did. She couldn't help but let out a joyous laugh at the unexpected move. The song was ending, and

King Luka dipped her, giving her a relaxed smile before returning her upright.

"You are a wonderful dancer." She said as they walked to the side.

"You are an enjoyable partner." He looked behind her, his face giving way to a knowing grin. "I mean no disrespect, but I am going to go mingle. Your valiant suitor approaches." He bowed, still holding her hand, placing a respectful kiss on the top before he walked away. Alveen spun around to see her handsome guard approaching.

"It is hard to keep eyes off you Princess." He stated. "You shine here tonight. Even among royalty, there is something about you."

"I believe it would be this gown and a skilled attendant that is very good with makeup." She joked.

"I don't think so." Samual looked down to Alveen's content face as she admired the crowd. A loose curl softly danced in the night breeze against her smooth cheek and her eyes glowed in the warm light around them, looking especially elegant this evening.

"Banphrionsa?" He whispered. She could swear he almost sounded nervous as her eyes met his. "May I have this dance?" Holding out his bent arm, he patiently waited as the next song began.

"Of course you may." She smiled brightly, enclosing his arm with hers as he led her towards the center of the clearing. "Be warned, I'm still not very good at this, especially in this gown.

Luka lead that whole last dance" He entwined his fingers into hers and softly placed his other hand at the small of her back. He admired her gown once more, simply smiling though he wanted to make a suggestive comment about the fit of it. She rested her other hand on his bicep.

"No need to worry my love, just follow my lead." Stepping forward she followed suit taking a step back until she was in perfect rhythm with him.

"You're a natural." She closed her eyes smiling. He pulled her closer, trying to give her a moment to relax among the busy schedule they had that day. He thought for a moment as they danced. "King Luka seems like a gentleman. I don't see him speak much though."

"He is quiet I suppose. Some people see it as a bit rude. I feel a great friendship will develop between us."

"I'm not sure friendship is what his intentions are." Samual was a jealous man, but as he stated, he knew others would try to win her affection, and as much as she tried to comfort him with confirmations, how could he really compare to a King?

"Actually..." She trailed off, not wanting to give too much of their conversation away. "He made it clear that's all he wants, especially since he realizes my heart is with another. He said that he came simply as an ally, he had no interest in even meeting me before." Samual stopped in his tracks midst all the couples.

"You are trying to trick me to make me feel better."

"He has no desire to court me, we spoke of it." Samual stared into her glowing teal eyes rimmed in gold, watching the candlelight dance across the shining surface, and flicker across the glitter in her eye makeup. Her eye lashes extended long, making every time she merely blinked seem more seductive to him.

"Just know… I would fight a King, or a Prince or even an army for you, Princess." She rested her head against his forehead. His words echoed in her mind.

The ground began to shake, and a strong wind burst into the clearing, confusing the occupants. "A portal." Samual recognized immediately. "Hurry, go to The Queen. Get out of this clearing." He pushed her to the side as he yelled. "Everyone off the field now!" he demanded guiding them off. "Guards! Gather the royals."

Alveen could hardly keep her balance. As the world below her shook violently, she fell to the ground. A large whirlwind appeared only feet from where her and Samual just stood. Samual now stood braced for attack, along with dozens of guards.

"Get them to the palace! We have no idea what is coming through!" Alveen looked around, The Banri, Queen Kathryn and the two Princesses from Ireill were being guided away from the clearing. The men, Queen Lovisa and Princess Willow stood braced for attack.

"Alveen!" Prince Viktor ran to her side helping her up. "You must get to the palace"

"Let her stay!" Princess Willow interjected. "We don't even know what's going on yet." Just as if she called for it, the portal pulsed with a blue light, and someone rolled to the ground in front of Samual. Everyone held their breath waiting for more, seeing who ruined the evening. Two of the guards grabbed the man that laid on the ground, pushing him to his knees in front of Samual. His clothes were filthy, he wore a leather chest harness, holding no weapons, his hair black, eyes glowing blue.

"Reveal your identity!" Samual yelled holding a sword to the man. The man shook, unable to speak.

"I...I....I..." he stuttered trying to get the words out. "They're coming! They're coming!" He screamed, still visibly shaking, tears strewn down his face.

The portal pulsed yet again, everyone tensed waiting for the next arrival. "Lock him up for questioning. Take him to the palace, immediately. Take Princess Alveen also. NOW." Samual ordered to the two guards and then to Sir Caspian. Caspian galloped to her.

"Princess, come with me." Alveen wanted to stay and fight, but she had little training and this gown was far too restricting. She grabbed his hand, allowing him to pull her up onto his back, making her get away hasty. She gripped onto his armor looking back to the field. Half a dozen more portals opened, raising tension in the air. Zakarian stood by Samual, awaiting the force behind the veil.

She glanced back to where Caspian was taking her directly down the village street, and more portals opened up. Within moments, Caspian slid to a halt.

"Alveen!!" Her friend screamed from behind her. Princess Willow now stood by her side. "I don't think you will make it to the palace." She stated obviously trying to make light of the terrible situation.

"I cannot fight like this." Willow looked her up and down.

"You're right, that won't work. Kick off your shows Princess." She did as instructed. "Now hold very still." Willow pulled out an arrow from the quiver that now graced her hip, finding the side seam, she pressed the broad head into the thread, ripping the gown high on her thigh and repeating it on the other side as well giving The Princess mobility at the very least. Alveen looked down shocked but impressed that there were no marks on her legs. "There." Princess Willow smiled broadly, turning back.

They turned back to back, Alveen facing the clearing, Willow and Caspian facing the portals between them and the palace. The Stench was the first thing that disclosed the truth about the invaders now diving through the portals. Syragons. More than just one or two this time, dozens. The rancid smell of burning flesh and rotten seaweed swirled through the many bodies readying for what was about to ensue.

"Princess?" Willow asked nervously.

"Yes?" Alveen's tone matching hers.

"I understand you have quite the access to magic. I suggest you try to pull that to the surface." Alveen faced her, seeing syragons approaching from the other side as well.

"Caspian! I need a weapon." He reached into his back holster, grabbing a dagger for her, that ended up being like a sword to her with their gracious size difference. She would need to find a new weapon fast. Without warning swords clashed. Willow was shoved aside by the first syragon, Caspian holding off three on his own.

The scene only repeated itself on the training grounds. Bodies flew with what looked like little force from the demonic creatures attacking her kingdom. She tried to dig deep but her nerves were far too distracted, there was too much going on. She swung, heart beating fast, at the syragon nearing her. He shoved her to the ground.

"This is too easy." He snarled, followed by a deafening shriek as Caspian drove a sword through its back, cutting off its wing, causing it to turn its attention to him. It approached Caspian, who was already sporting splatters of blood from the two syragons that laid dead on the street. She sat back, thinking of the best way to approach the situation. An idea sprung in her head, she just wasn't sure if she could execute it.

She charged towards Caspian silently, although she was certain every person could hear her heart beating even through the battle clatter. Swinging the sword, she missed the arm of the beast, falling towards Caspian her sword screeched across his armor, producing the smallest spark and once she saw it, she shot her arm out towards the creature and let the gate down holding the magic within her. Her skin felt warm and she felt renewed as the smallest spark burst forth into a rolling flame, engulfing the monster, leaving him shrieking as he burned.

"Thank-You Princess." Caspian said to her, looking into the same glowing eyes she had during her first encounter. She nodded to him, ready to fight for her kingdom.

~Chapter XVII~

The Battle

Alveen couldn't be more thankful to Willow for her ability to move right now. She ran to her side after she was knocked down.

"Willow! Are you alright?"

"It takes a lot more than getting smacked around to end this Princess." She spoke fiercely. "However, they just might have me outdone this time." She admitted looking around to the incoming army of beasts. "We need a strategy." Alveen thought back to her training. She had begun reading about strategizing and battle formations. Nothing came to mind immediately, all she had to go on was her limited knowledge. "Do you have any perches? Anywhere I can be out of reach and we can see what's going on?" Alveen thought about the answer to Willows questions.

"Follow me." She pulled Willow to her feet and ran towards the clearing, ducking into one of the building she knew had an interior staircase through the healing room, so they wouldn't be seen. As they entered the room Alveen was healed in, they ran to the doorway, observing the battle below. The portals closed on the streets, giving Caspian the advantage over the field as he charged through, slamming into intruders King Hunter was battling.

"Only four portals left. Do you know how to close a portal? Can we even close them?" Alveen questioned Willow. Alveen was still learning but Willow should be well versed.

"We could but it would take a ton of energy, I'm not sure anyone here could do that."

"So, what do we do?" Before the question even left her lips, Willow's eyes lit up with an idea.

"I'm going to hop on the roof and shoot from above. I know you are powerful Alveen. Concentrate.."

"And do what? How do I kill these things?"

"You've done it before, just focus." Without another word, Willow hopped gracefully onto the railing and flipped onto the roof. She stared at a candle and reached her arm out and pulled a flame toward her, catching her arrow on fire as she flung it into the air. Alveen watched as it perfectly pierced the center of the monster's spine, immobilizing it. Killing it. Alveen could do this.

She took in a deep breath and started following Willows example. She reached both her hands to the flames in the hovering candles and after she felt that she had control over it, she forced it to snake down onto the battle field between Prince Viktor and two oncoming small syragons. The flame continued crawling around their claws, growing higher, swallowing them until only a pile of ash was left. Prince Viktor stood in astonishment.

"Whoa! I told you you could do it!" Willow yelled from the roof. Viktor flashed her a smile, racing to aid his father. Her confidence sky rocketed with the approval of her peers. She looked down to the field, seeing Luka surrounded by four enemies. Her arms shot out forcefully and she blew into the air. She could feel the wind as she forced it into two minor tornados, lifting the four off the ground into the tunnels. Their talons grasped at their throats as the breath left their lungs and the life faded from their eyes. Luka glanced at her and without a smile or nod, continued to push in against the monsters.

There were still dozens left. She slammed two together with a forceful gust. Two portals remained open and they seemed to be still outnumbered, even with their vast guard.

"Willow!" Alveen yelled. She was too absorbed in her own focus that she didn't hear her. Without being able to get an answer, she tested a theory twirling in her mind. She controlled air again, pushing back a large Syragon. His claw dug into the dirt below him, a mighty roar bellowed out as he fought against her. She pushed and forced more energy out. She could feel it exhausting her. She could feel him fighting her. Samual must have seen her and caught onto her idea, he barreled toward it and with one force filled kick, the monster released the ground and was sucked back into the portal.

Their eyes met for a moment. He smiled at her genius. She dropped her hands, trying to rest for only a moment. Samual walked towards her, the light of the portal to his back still. Zakarian approached him from the side, falling in line with him towards Alveen.

A cry erupted and Samual's eyes grew in size, no longer looking at Alveen but staring at his long-time best friend. Zakarian stood there with his sword through Samual's abdomen; his eyes filled with....nothing. They were empty, no regret, no sorrow.

She sat in disbelief for a split second before she stood, rushing down the stair case to Samual's side.

"NOO!!" She wailed in sorrow as tears began to swell up. Zakarian retreated as he saw her. He backed up and using the very magic he taught her, he reached out, stealing the air from around her. She slowed, gasping, still trying to reach Samual's body that now lay limp on the ground he trained so many others to fight on.

Her brother. The one person she grew up trusting, the one she remembered and loved betrayed her and their kingdom. As she stared at him, a figure emerged from the forest behind him, in a cloak so she couldn't see the person's face. He would not win this. Her grief swelled in her chest, her limbs began to feel a frosty chill.

She flicked her wrist, tossing Zakarian to the side with her last bit of energy as she crawled to Samual's body. His eyes lay closed, his chest wasn't moving. Queen Lovisa was by her side in an instant. Checking for any sign of life.

"Princess. He's gone. There is no saving him now." She didn't believe it. Her heart pounded in her head.

"Get everyone away. Now!" She screamed to The Queen. Had anyone else said this The Queen would have thought them foolish, but when Alveen's face turned to her, her eyes glowed fiercely, and she was emerged in this battle as her magic was spilling over. Queen Lovisa had never seen anything like that before, and took her warning ordering the other royals, guards and citizens to take cover.

"Retreat!" She screamed, letting out a long whistle to rally in the royals and the guards that remained. Alveen took in a deep breath feeling as if she inhaled icicles. The sharp pain in her chest welled up and as she exhaled, leaning over Samual's body, Zakarian stood back up with the stranger in tow.

"NOOOOOOOOOOO!!" As the word left her throat in an angry scream, the icy feeling inside her exploded outward, rippling through the remaining creatures standing in the clearing and in the street. She heard the cracking of their bones as the force of her heartache thrust through their bodies. "WHAT HAVE YOU DONE?" she screamed after her brother who was walking towards the portal with a protective hand up holding a shield that would give way any second against her power. He was now holding the stranger's hand and before the last ripple of her angish could tear them a part the stranger dropped her hood and held Alveen's stare for a split second. Alveen recognized the glowing pink eyes of Malika following him into the portal. The final ripple was enough to close the last entrance.

Alveen lay alone, in silence, as the smoke around her cleared and people began to emerge from where they hid. She rested her shaking hand on Samual's cheek as she fell unconscious.

Alveen heard her name being called as she came back to counsiousness. She did not black out very long since she was still in the middle of the field the battle was just fought. She opened her eyes momentarily to see guards were hauling bodies away and cleaning up the rubble.

"Princess? Alveen? Are you with me? Are you alright?" the deep voice rumbled her chest. She opened her eyes again, seeing golden eyes looking down at her, feeling muscular arms wrapped around her body. "Princess?" He said one more time.

"Luka?" she asked dazed.

"Yes, Princess. Oh, Snowfall you're alright." He pulled her close.

"Yes, it would be tragic if I perished. Your only friend would be gone." She said sarcastically. She felt him laugh as he held her, helping her sit up. As she looked around, she began to remember what happened. "Samual." She said, dropping all jokes and feeling her heart swell with ache again. "Where is Samual?" She frantically asked him. Princess Willow approaches.

"Oh, great vines she's alive!"

"Where's Samual? Why won't you...." She stopped looking at the spot next to her. His body no longer lay there, but the blood was very real and the story finished itself in her mind. Tears fell hot down her cheeks.

"Alveen, I'm so sorry. The healers even tried. There was nothing they could do." Willow said. She moved closer, wrapping her arms around her. "I don't say this to be discourteous or to minimize the severity of the situation, but you should know, you are not the only one who lost someone today."

Alveen sat up. "How many did we lose?"

"Total? Over forty." She paused before she hesitantly continued. "Two were royals." Alveen tried to quickly get to her feet. King Luka sat by silently, helping her to stand. She walked over to where they were collecting the dead. Prince Viktor was down on his knees, Princess Willow, King Luka and Princess Alveen standing behind him, all covered in their own pattern of blood and dirt hardening across their skin, grieving the guards, the citizens and the two lost royals, King Bowen and King Ronan, who laid dead on the ground in front of them.

THE STORY CONTINUES WITH:

BREWING BATTLES

~Chapter 1~

Grieving for Cosaint

"The stranger! The one you took to be questioned, where is he?" The Princess lividly roared at the first guard she met as she entered the palace. She had never demanded anything of anyone, but that was before the man she loved was murdered, her kingdom was attacked during a sacred event and her brother betrayed her family. She needed to speak with him and find out what he knew. The guard before her looked terrified. Alveen was still in her black gown, sliced up the side and covered in various patterns of dried mud from the battle only hours ago. Her hair a mess and her eyes glowing with anger, she would find out why this happened.

"Your Highness, I do not know. I was not informed. I swear." Alveen stared at him for a moment before moving past him to meet with The Queen. She made her way to the throne room with haste, hoping to find her grandmother there. She passed the towering guards who stood tall in her presence.

"Where is he?" She asked simply, her face hard as stone, as she pushed open the metallic golden doors that gave way to the vast display of tree trunk pillars and floating vines. The only light from that which the canopy above allowed in. There was a boundary spell around the castle, so even though many of the ceilings were open to the sky, the elements would not penetrate it. The Queen stood with her back to the door, clean as can be. She and a few other royals were rushed to the palace before the battle began, Alveen was caught in the middle, unable to escape and forced to fight for her life, which it turned out she was more skilled at than even she would have ever guessed.

"Who?" The Queen simply asked, still not facing her.

"The stranger. The one they brought back to the palace to question. I want to question him too."

"Alveen." The Queen scoffed, "What do you possibly think you will be able to ask that we can't?" Her heart raced.

"I may not be able to say anything that you all can't, but I promise I can be a most persuading interrogator if necessary." Her voice was at a near growl.

"I will not allow you anywhere near the stranger until I first question him, and you learn to control your emotions." She spun around so fast her gown had to catch up with her. Her face was frustrated. "You are a Princess and you will not be torn apart by these emotions. You will lose control faster than you have the ability to fix your mistakes." She was slowly walking towards the tattered-up Princess.

"He has the answers. He is responsible for Samual's death!" She screamed, tears threatening once again to spill onto her blood-spattered cheeks.

"No." The Queen raised her voice but remained in control. "That man is not responsible for anyone's death. Zakarian alone is responsible for the death of Samual, though I can imagine it's easier to blame a stranger verse your own brother whom you've trusted your entire life." She was being blunt to Alveen. "As a Queen, there is no room for self-pity or for personal emotion and being the last heir to this throne, Alveen you will have to learn that very quickly."

Alveen dropped to the floor on her cut up knees, cupping her face in her hands to hide the crimson color her face was turning as the pain of loss over whelmed her. "He's gone." She cried.

"Yes. He is." The Queen stated. "So are over thirty others, two of which were kings if you happen to have forgotten that." She knelt down to her granddaughter, pulling her hands away so she could look her in the eyes. Her eyes were glowing as she met the Queen's stare, so much anger in the peridot lights. "Alveen, Viktor just lost his father and Karolyn her brother. Those guards? They had families also." She pulled Alveen to her feet. "I know you will not like hearing this, but this is not about you. If you ever wish to be a great ruler, you must learn to put your loss and your struggles behind you and focus on those of your kingdom and of your allies. Don't let Samual be followed into death by you because you cannot control yourself." The

Princess stood there silent, unable to talk and think. "Now if you're ready to reign in your anger, I will speak with you in regard to the matter you came here for." Alveen took a deep breath, swallowing the truth her grandmother just laid out in front of her. She tried to relax.

"What have you found out?"

"I'm sorry to say, very little. He claims to not know his name, not know anything about his past. He said all he remembers is waking up in front of a sorceress. He was meant to be held captive, but he escaped the grips of one of the tribe members and dove through their open portal before they entered, and all he knew was that he had to warn us."

"What good that did." She stated. "Do you believe him?"

"I do. I believe it is more than possible the sorceress held him captive and wiped his memory."

"You don't recognize him?"

"Not at all. He has a very different mix of features I've never seen before." The Queen looked at her granddaughter. "I am truly sorry for your loss my dear. I did not mean to sound so insensitive. Samual had come to me only days ago asking to court you so I understand the nature of your relationship." She placed a hand on her shoulder. "And I am only trying to help you gain control because you have now moved to the top of the line as heir to the Cosaint throne. Should anything happen to me, you must lead our kingdom." Alveen hadn't even thought about that. With Zakarian betraying his kingdom he forfeited his right to the throne.

"I don't understand what he did." The Princess stated, focusing on the floor in front of her.

"I have an assumption." She walked back to her throne, gently lowering herself onto the branches that entwined to make the elaborate seat. "Were you aware of his relationship? And that there was a child of it?"

"I was, I have seen her only a number of times, but I have never spoken to her. She was with him. When he betrayed us." The Queen nodded.

"Yes. He had come to me only shortly after Samual did, begging for me to accept his relationship with Malika and to accept his child. I refused." She tapped her finger on the arm of the throne. "So, I suppose it can be in part blamed on me."

"Why would that cause him to betray his kingdom? And me?"

"Simple. There are no rules in the Dorcha tribes. There is no structure. I rejected for the pure reason of not trusting her, it had nothing to do with her race, though I'm certain he assumed otherwise." The little girl with straight blonde hair and glowing pink eyes entered her mind.

"What of Tanilly? Did they take her with them?"

"Surprisingly not. The guards found her only a short while ago. She is resting in my chambers."

"What will come of her? Her parents abandoned her. She has no one."

"I'm very much aware of that. I have decided that she will be in my care until further notice. The world still believes in a truly pure elven monarch, so though she is Zakarian's heir, it will be a battle to get her rights to the throne, one I fear I may not be able to win." She sighed. "But that will come later. For now, we must ensure she is safe, and not allow her father's decisions to affect her life. I will begin schooling her after the memorial services."

www.ingramcontent.com/pod-product-compliance
Lightning Source LLC
Chambersburg PA
CBHW020547020726
47494CB00006B/1958